R.W. Ridley

The Land of the Dead

Book Four of the Oz Chronicles

Single 'R' Imprint
Middlebury House Publishing,
Printed in USA

ISBN10: 0-9792067-3-1
ISBN13: 978-0-9792067-3-3
Library of Congress Control Number: Pending

To order additonal copies, please contact the distributor.
Middleburry House Publishing
MidPub@yahoo.com

Names, characters, places, and incidents are the products of the author's imagination or are used fictionally. Any resemblance to actual events, locales, or persons, living or dead, is entirely coincidental.

Printed in the United States of America.

10 9 8 7 6 5 4 3 2 1
First Edition

The Land of the Dead

Book Four of the Oz Chronicles

Books for Young Adults by R.W. Ridley

Oz Chronicles Titles

Book One - The Takers

Book Two - Délon City

Book Three - The Pure

Book Four - The Land of the Dead

Non-Oz Titles

Lost Days

For Mia. Thanks for being my one true love.

ONE

I died when I was eleven. It was a family vacation on Oak Island, North Carolina, extended family, cousins, aunts, uncles, grandparents, even a foreign exchange student from France. My cousin Anthony and I swam out past a sandbar scaring the crap out of each other by yelling shark every five minutes. We screamed and laughed and drifted along the shoreline. That's when it hit us. A current, I think they call it a riptide, sucked us off our feet and started carrying us farther out from shore. We both panicked. I kicked and sputtered across the surface of the water, swimming against the current. My breathing was quick and shallow. I grunted and pounded my arms on the choppy surface of the ocean. I looked to my left where Anthony had been and all I saw was the top of his head as he went under. I opened my mouth to call his name but I sucked in a mouthful of salt water, causing me to hack and cough as if my lungs were trying to burst out of my body. Anthony resurfaced. In between gasps, he managed to yell for help. I tried to do the same but only swallowed more water. My arms felt like lead weights. I felt myself sinking. I attempted to fight harder, but I didn't have the strength. I tilted my head back, keeping my nose out of the water, and tried to breathe through my mouth. The water flooded my lungs. I couldn't even gasp. A searing pain, as if my breast bone was about to crack open, was the last thing I remember before everything went dark.

I was dead.

I don't know how long it was before they revived me. I was lying on my side on the beach. The foreign exchange student had her finger in my mouth shouting, "Ee is breeding! Ee is alive!"

It felt like I was spewing a couple of gallons of water. My chest still felt like it was going to split open.

I heard mom's voice. "Oz! Oh my God, Oz!" Her knees popped as she knelt down beside me. She gently placed her hand on top of my head. "Sweet baby."

"Where's Anthony?" I heard someone ask. I think it was my Aunt Sadie, Anthony's mother.

I didn't hear anyone answer her.

"Where's Anthony?" she repeated, a little more shrill than before.

"They're looking." The voice belonged to my cousin Johnny. His too-deep voice gave him away. He was the oldest and vastly most bored of the Griffin kids, and he usually talked with a dull cadence, but now he sounded defensive and scared.

"Who's looking... for what?" Aunt Sadie asked breathlessly.

An answer came after a long pause.

"Anthony," Johnny said. "He's in the water."

He said it without saying it. Anthony had gone under. He'd drowned. He was dead like me, but unlike me, they wouldn't be able revive him. It would be hours before they even found him.

Until the world ended, that was pretty much my worst day.

***

I am responsible for the end of the world. Well, me and every other jerk like me who tortured the Storytellers. Only we didn't know they were Storytellers then. They were... different than us, slow, dumb, retarded. We didn't think they deserved to be treated like human beings so we treated them like something less than human. But we were the ones being less than human. We ridiculed them and shamed them until all they saw was a world with monsters. They wrote stories about those monsters. Drew pictures. Created comic books. Eventually the monsters crawled out of the comic books and drawings and destroyed the world.

It doesn't seem real. How could it be? Monsters, Storytellers... It can't be, can it? Even though I live it every day, it's hard for me to believe it. Some doctor... a psychiatrist I think, taught the Storytellers to think things to life. He called it Hyper Mental Imaging. That's how all this happened. Some shrink, Dr. Bashir, caused all this. He is responsible...

No. I am responsible for the end of the world.

***

I sat on a rusted metal folding chair under the shabby awning of an abandoned BP convenience store. My muscles ached. My feet throbbed. My hands were cramped from my constant nervous habit of clenching them. All of this was just background noise in my head. I was only faintly aware of it. My focus was on my parents.

I missed them. I had not seen them in... I had no idea how much time had passed since I last saw them. It was in Atlanta... Délon City. In the Georgia Dome... No, wait. I couldn't count that time. They weren't them. Not exactly. They were... in transition. My father more so than my mother, but neither of them was human... more Délon than human.

The last time I really saw them, when they were human and the sky was blue and there were no purple freaks or Takers or... pick your hellish monster. The last time was in Tullahoma. I was sick in bed with mono. I was so hot I was cold. I remember their worried faces. My mother stroked my forehead and cried. My dad rubbed his stubbly chin with his callused hand. This meant he was scared. My mother had told me that once when I was younger, six maybe. He had just gotten the news that his mother had passed away. He hung up the phone and stared at the wall, rubbing his chin.

"He's scared," my mother said. She sat me in her lap and allowed me to watch my father from afar. For some reason it was important for me to see him at that moment. It was new to me. I had never seen him like that before. It concerned me, and yet fascinated me. "It's okay, Oz. Scared is good. Scared means we're confused. And we find confused right before we get to where we need to be. Do you know where that is, Oz? Where we need to be?"

I shook my head.

"Understanding," she said. "We all need to understand. So you let your Pop be scared. He's just trying to understand."

It meant nothing to me at the time, but sitting in an unsteady chair on the cracked pavement of the BP station, with black continents of clouds creeping overhead, and watching a Twix candy wrapper dance in a whirling stale wind, I knew exactly what she'd meant. Only I wasn't sure there was ever a time I was actually going to understand what was happening to me, to my friends, to my world. I felt perpetually confused. There couldn't possibly be any good in that.

I groaned as I repositioned myself in the chair. I did not think it possible to feel so entirely sore. I lifted my aching arm to rub my stiff neck and caught a glimpse of a girl I barely recognized. She was staring at me from one of the defunct gas pumps. It was Lou, but it wasn't. I was not used to seeing her like this... she wasn't a little kid anymore. She was a full-fledged teenager. The wind blew her hair across her face. And suddenly I was struck by the notion that she was... pretty.

She brushed the hair from her face. "You can't do that again, you know," she said.

I didn't answer right away. I was in the middle of trying to decide if I liked her being pretty.

"Hey," she said. "You hear me?"

"Yeah, I heard," I said breaking eye contact with her. "Don't know what you're talking about though."

"Leave," she said stepping off the pump island and strolling closer. "You were gone too long. Things nearly went all to pot. I didn't like it much... that is to say, we didn't like it much."

"I wasn't that thrilled about it myself."

"Lost Valerie," she said. I heard her voice break on the last syllable.

"I know. It wasn't your fault."

She took a deep breath and squeaked out, "Kinda was." Her eyes welled up.

"We lost plenty on my watch," I said. "Soldiers die in wars."

"She was just a kid." She dropped her chin to her chest and shook her head back and forth slowly. "You can't leave again," she said, almost begging now.

I stood and approached her. "I promise, Lou. I'm never leaving you... all again."

She sniffed and nodded. "We missed you."

"Yeah," I said. I fought the urge to reach out and pat her shoulder.

"Ain't much in there," Wes said, exiting the building. He cradled a load of mix-and-match snacks against his protruding belly. "Pretzels, peanuts, cheese and crackers, pork rinds... couple of Twinkies. One of them is mine," he said.

Gordy appeared from behind him favoring his wounded shoulder. Lou had dressed it, but it would need changing soon. "That's a surprise," Gordy said. "You like Twinkies?"

"Boy," Wes said, "you been gone all this time and you're going to start in on me?"

"I'm just saying that's all."

He took the cheese and crackers and held it up. "Y'all mind if I have this?"

Lou and I shook our heads.

He tore the wrapper with his teeth and hurriedly devoured the snack.

Ajax lumbered over to us from the corner of the store, followed by Kimball. It was good to see my best gorilla and my best dog again. I had forgotten how much I missed them. I took the remaining Twinkie and tossed it to Ajax. He grinned and nodded his massive head in excitement.

Kimball whined. I called him over and tore open a bag of pork rinds. I gave him one of the fried fatty treats. He crunched it tentatively at first and then quickly decided that he loved the taste of it. I dumped the rest of the rinds on the pavement. He pounced on them with reckless abandon.

I turned to Lou, holding the peanuts in one hand and the pretzels in the other. She snatched the pretzels from me.

"One thing's for sure," Wes said. "This ain't going to be nearly enough to keep up our strength. I feel weak as a kitten."

Gordy laughed. "Lord, Wes, if you don't want me to make fun of you, you gotta stop saying things like that."

Wes looked at me. "Can we send him back?"

I smiled and shook my head back and forth. "Like it or not, we need him."

"Gee thanks," Gordy said.

"Got any ideas where we're headed?" Wes asked.

I popped some peanuts into my mouth. "Playing it by ear."

"What about Tyrone and April?" Lou asked staring at a pretzel.

I searched for the perfect answer. The truth is I didn't have much hope they were alive. They got separated from the rest of us and were in the middle of a pack of Myrmidons. I didn't think it mattered much that I had sent Ariabod and another gorilla to look for them. They wouldn't find them. In fact, the gorillas were probably dead, too. "Can't worry about them." It wasn't perfect, but it was honest.

"What do you mean?" Wes asked.

"I mean they're in good hands with Ariabod," I lied. "He's a great warrior. They'll find us no matter where we go." Ajax confirmed my statement with a nod and grin.

A strong wind whipped through the small parking area. Dust and debris swept across the asphalt. I looked down as an old brochure slammed into my leg. I kicked, trying to work it free so it could go on its merry way, but it wouldn't come loose. I bent down and grabbed it with the intention of tossing it aside. Instead, four letters caught my attention: Bilt. I looked closer at the trifold brochure. Biltmore House. I must have said it out loud because Lou asked me what I'd said.

I cleared my throat. "Biltmore House, in Ashville. My mom always wanted to go there. Dad promised her we'd go."

Wes grabbed the brochure from me. "Biltmore, huh? Yeah, I heard of the place. Mansion. Castle, really. Built by the Vanderbilts I think."

Lou approached, fixated on the photo of the Biltmore House. "It's beautiful. How far is it from here?"

Wes thought about the question. He surveyed the road in front of the convenience store. "Two days' walk, maybe less."

"Let's go," Lou said.

"What?" I said, sounding a little indigent. "We don't have time to sightsee."

"Really?" she said. "And why not? You said yourself you don't know where we're going."

"Well yeah, but…"

"We need some time to figure it out," she said. "We might as well figure it out in a pretty place."

"We have to find the Land of the Dead," I said.

She snickered. "It's going to find us. You know that better than anyone."

She was right. I shrugged my shoulders, and she smiled. It was all the happy she could muster. Visiting a genuine American castle was small consolation when things like castles and America didn't matter anymore.

I thought about my parents again and realized that it wasn't just them who were dead. The entire world was dead. Maybe we didn't have to find the Land of the Dead. Maybe we were already in it.

The sky began to rumble and roar. Flashes of lightning burst over our heads.

"We should sit this out in the store," Wes said.

No one argued. I was the last one to step inside the convenience store. As soon as I did, a torrent of rain fell and beat the metal building mercilessly.

"Bad," Gordy said.

"Ain't much good about anything for a while now," Wes replied.

I turned to him. There was something in his tone... he was done. Defeated. I didn't like the sound of it... I hated it. "You're alive," I said suppressing a visible display of anger.

He huffed as if it were the most ridiculous thing he had ever heard.

"What?" I asked stepping toward him.

"Ain't enough, that's all."

"What is enough?"

He looked up at the ceiling and absorbed the unnaturally heavy sound of the rain. "A sunny day." He looked at me. "You know? A real day. A yellow sun. A blue sky. Puffy white clouds." Without warning, he kicked a rack of pine-scented air fresheners. "While you're at it, I'd like to see my sister, and her good-for-nothing husband, and Pepper..." He looked at Lou. "And Valerie."

Lou bit her lip and looked away.

A crack of thunder shook the foundation of the convenience store.

"You will..."

"Stop it, Oz!" Wes roared. The power of his voice sent a heat wave through the tiny store. "Just stop!"

No one spoke for several minutes. We all were trying to understand Wes's sudden outburst. Even Wes.

Finally he spoke in much softer tones. "I'm tired..."

"We all are," I said.

"No," he said, "let me finish. I'm tired of hoping for things that ain't never going to happen. We gotta stop this foolishness."

"Foolishness?" I said.

"That's right, foolishness. We can't go back."

I looked at the faces of the others. They were stunned by his words. "Yes, we can."

"No, we can't," Wes said. "We are being hunted down by... monsters."

"Destroyers," Gordy corrected him.

"Whatever you want to call them. They're in charge. This ain't our world no more. We need to face that and..."

"Do what?" I asked. "What good will it do for us to just give up?"

"It will keep us off the warpath for one thing," Wes said.

"No," Lou said. "It won't. They'll keep coming after us. We can't quit this."

"That might not be true," Wes said.

"What do you mean?" I asked.

"The Délons are losing control."

"So," I said.

"So I figure they will be fightin' among themselves soon enough. All of them. Délons, Myrmidons, Silencers, Takers, Bashirs. They won't have time to fool with us. I say we head up North. Find a nice cold spot to lay low. Let the monsters wipe each other out."

"Won't work," Lou said. "Oz is the key to finding their source."

"No I'm not."

"They think you are," Lou said. "That means you are."

Wes looked at me. He wanted to say something, but he didn't. He shrugged his shoulders. "I'm just having a bad day. Y'all don't pay no attention to me." He walked to the window behind the counter and watched the rain.

I stepped to the opposite end of the store, bothered more by what Wes didn't say than by what he did. They were all better off without me.

TWO

By the time the rain let up, nightfall was upon us. We decided to wait it out until morning to begin our trek to the Biltmore House. We slept in shifts. I volunteered to take the first watch with Gordy. Lou was hurt. She wanted to spend some time alone with me, but we would talk strategy, and losses, and feelings. I wasn't in the mood for those conversations.

Gordy and I set up two chairs behind the register. Earlier, we had found a case of energy drinks in the manager's office so we popped a couple open and sipped on the tangy drinks. They were awful, but they kept us bright-eyed so they served their purpose.

"How's your brain?" Gordy asked.

"Huh? My brain?"

"Dude, that shunter worked on you for a long time."

"Oh." I reached up and felt my temples. "I'm a little fuzzy. Kind of feels like I just woke up from a deep sleep all the time."

"I'd kill for that feeling," he said. He downed the last drop of his energy drink and tossed the can in a nearby trashcan. "You know what I really miss?"

I shook my head.

"Cheeseburgers. Big, thick, juicy cheeseburgers. Melted cheese, tomato. Slice of bacon." He leaned back. "Oh, man. I'd fight a thousand wars to get back home and sink my teeth into a cheeseburger."

"Pizza for me, man," I said. "Sausage, hamburger, and onion. Thick crust. Big cold glass of Coke. Crushed ice."

"Bread sticks," Gordy said. "Gotta have bread sticks."

"With garlic butter dipping sauce."

"Sweet," Gordy said.

We both relaxed in our chairs and savored our imaginary meals. I think I may have even smiled. I breathed in deeply as if I could smell the melted cheese of my make-a-wish pizza.

"Dessert," Gordy said. "What about it?"

"Shake," I said. "Vanilla with a little cream soda mixed in. Something my dad used to make. Made it so thick, you'd have to eat it with a spoon. He called it heaven in a glass. He was a hundred percent right, too. It was."

"Brownie for me," Gordy said. "Hot, chewy, thick, chocolaty. The smell... it's like fresh... Man, I can taste it now."

We both relaxed, and didn't take notice of it. If we had, we would have realized how absolutely special it was. The tension was gone. The fear was gone. The worry... gone.

I leaned back in my chair. "What's something you don't miss?"

"Huh?" Gordy said.

"Seems like all we talk about is the stuff that was fun. There's gotta be something you don't miss."

Gordy thought. "I don't think there is."

"C'mon."

He shook his head. "Seriously. I can't think of nothing that's worse than this. I mean my old man could get mean when he drank. My little sister was a royal pain most of the time, and I hated Mrs. Hurley's little dog. Thing bit me three times. But I swear on a stack of Bibles I'd let that damn thing bite me a hundred times a day if it meant I could go home."

I nodded. "Yeah, I guess it was a stupid question."

Gordy shrugged. "I gotta admit it's kind of nice not having to go to Ms. Paul's house for piano lessons. She smelled funny."

I chuckled. "I didn't know you were taking piano lessons."

"Just started. My mom made me. Wanted me to get some culture. Not even sure what that means."

"I think it means not telling people Ms. Paul smelled funny."

He waved me off. "Then culture ain't for me." He stood. "I gotta pee."

I set my energy drink on the floor. "I'll go with you."

"I can pee by myself," he said.

"I don't plan on helping you," I said. "I just don't want you to go outside alone."

He thought it over and then nodded.

We moved around the counter and quietly pulled the door open. I took a quick look at the others. They were snoozing away. It was good to see.

Outside, Gordy headed for the pumps while I wandered to the curb.

"Tell you one thing I miss," Gordy said.

"What's that?" I asked as I strained to see as far as I could down the dark stretch of road.

"A working toilet."

The wind picked up. Black clouds raced across a dark purple sky. A grunt soared up out of the darkness, followed by a high-pitched wail. A girl screamed. I had no weapon. I turned to warn the others and was startled to see Ajax approaching. He bore a grim look on his face.

"Crap!" Gordy barked. "That doesn't sound good."

Ajax knuckle-walked into the middle of the road.

"What is it?" I asked him.

He beat his chest.

A girl ran out of the dark horizon of the road. She was

shrieking at the top of her lungs.

Gordy joined me at the curb.

"Who's that?" he asked.

"April," I said. I don't know how I knew it was her. I had never met her. I had only heard Archie talk about her. I suppose I just assumed it was her.

Tyrone appeared shortly after.

"Ty!" Gordy yelled.

We both followed Ajax as he bolted towards them. In retrospect, it probably wasn't a smart thing to do. His hair was up. He was running into a fight. Neither Gordy nor I had a weapon of any kind. I turned to my right and saw Kimball race by us. It wasn't long before he was hot on the heels of his old friend Ajax.

Gordy and I reached April and Tyrone. "You okay?"

"Oz!" Tryone shouted. I had forgotten we hadn't seen each other in a very long time. He hugged me. I couldn't believe how tall he was.

"Ty, good to see you, little man."

He pushed himself back. "We gotta get out of here."

"Why?" Gordy asked.

A lone Myrmidon stepped out of the dark horizon. It was enormous . . . ten feet tall. It wore black thick armor from head to toe.

April shrieked, "That's why."

Gordy gasped. "Why do they always have to be so big?"

"Ajax!" I yelled.

The silverback ignored me. He raced for the Myrmidon. The giant ant-man crouched and readied itself for Ajax's attack. I turned to Gordy. "Get them back to the store."

"What are you going to do?"

"I don't know yet." I turned and chased after Ajax. As I ran, I scanned both sides of the road for something I could use as a weapon. It was amazingly clear of debris.

Ajax had stopped twenty feet from the Myrmidon. He stood and pounded his chest. Kimball barked and growled. The Myrmidon screeched. Out of the darkness, a flash of silver and black launched itself through the air and landed on the back of the Myrmidon. Ariabod. The huge silverback knocked the ant-man to the ground and brought his large fists down on the creature's helmeted head. The Myrmidon was unaffected. He tossed Ariabod aside like a stuffed animal and jumped to his feet. Ajax leapt forward and swept the giant's legs out from under it before it had time to react. The ground shook when the Myrmidon hit the pavement. Ajax stood on its chest. Kimball nipped at the monster and looked for a soft spot to bite. Ariabod found his balance and joined Ajax in the fight. Together, the two gorillas thrashed the Myrmidon with their fists. Each blow was quick and fierce. They were relentless. I heard the creature's bones break. It twitched and wheezed as it was being beaten to death. The two gorillas would not stop. They were driven by a kind of madness that frightened me. I almost felt sorry for the Myrmidon.

It wasn't long before the Myrmidon didn't move on its own. It was clearly dead yet the two silverbacks continued to pound it with their fists.

"Ajax, stop." I said much too quietly.

Ariabod stopped. He grunted and huffed erratically as he plodded away from the body. Ajax continued to pummel the dead Myrmidon. The creature's bones crunched as they fractured under the stress of Ajax's powerful blows.

"Ajax!" I yelled.

He turned to me. His eyes were wide open, and his fangs showed as his mouth was stretched in an awful grimace. He breathed heavily. He looked at me, but I was sure he couldn't see me. He was gone. Lost in his rage.

I stuck my hands up, palms down. "Easy." Kimball had backed away at this point. He sat with his head cocked to the side, studying his old friend.

Slowly, the grimace relaxed. Ajax climbed off the Myrmidon's chest and was greeted by a sloppy tongue to the face from Kimball. The two were joined by Ariabod and they all headed toward the store. I took a step toward the Myrmidon and studied its battered body. I heard footsteps approaching. I turned to see Wes standing behind me.

"Dead?" he asked standing at what he deemed to be a safe distance while craning his neck to get a better look.

"So far," I said.

"Any more out there?"

I shook my head. "I don't think so."

"Why don't you think so?"

"Hunch. I get the feeling they're not built for going solo. I'm guessing there were more of them, but Ariabod disposed of them somehow. If there were others, they'd be here by now."

He scratched his stubbly check. "You got these things figured out pretty quick."

"Not that hard." I squatted and stared at the corpse. "You don't want me here do you, Wes?"

"What?" I could feel him staring at me. "Son, I will kick your ass from here to China if you say something like that again."

"It's okay. I get it. I'm putting everyone in danger."

"Is this about me going off before?"

I didn't answer.

"Look here, this is a hard life, Oz. I ain't always going to be... positive about this path we've chosen. I got weak. That's all." I heard him sniffle. "You're my family, you and the others. I'd just as soon lay down my own life than see you leave us again. And Miss Lou... She'd go stark raving mad. I can't have that."

I stood and turned. I saw a tear slide down his fat cheek.

He cleared his throat. "I need you, boy."

I smiled and we headed back to the store.

***

"Three took out after us," Tyrone said. "Ariabod and Jambo, the other gorilla, held them off for a while... and then Jambo... they got him, but he took one out. Broke that sucker's neck. We outran them, or at least we thought we did. They caught up to us a few miles back. Attacked us while we were sleeping. Ariabod done one in, and April and me took off. Ended up here."

"The other apes?" I asked.

Ariabod signed while Lou interpreted.

"He says they're out there. Waiting."

"Waiting for what?" Gordy asked.

Ariabod signed.

"War... something," Lou said.

The gorilla signed again.

Frustrated, she said, "Signing faster doesn't help. It's war... something. That's the best I can do."

"Unless the rest of it is 'War ain't happening,' I don't want to hear it anyway," Gordy said.

"Where's Archie?" April asked. She was sipping away on an energy drink.

"Didn't make it," Gordy said.

I shot him a look. "We don't know that for sure." I tried to give April a reassuring smile.

"Those giant bad guys in black armor say different," Gordy said.

"Could be the Keeper died for all we know," I said. "Nothing more."

"I don't understand," April said, lip trembling, shoulders

shaking.

"Whenever awarrior ...," Gordy started.

"Creyshaw," I said.

"Fine, Creyshaw. Whenever a Creyshaw fails and a Storyteller is captured by the Destroyers, a new race of Destroyers comes forward."

"From where?" April asked.

"From the North Pole, Never Never Land, Atlantis, who knows."

"Some of them also come forward if the Keeper dies," I said.

"Maybe," Gordy said.

"Bobby said..." I started.

"Bobby said. Bobby said. Bobby had half the sense of a brainless bat," Gordy responded.

"Y'all are doing a lot of yapping about stuff that don't matter a lick," Wes said. "We need to rest up and get ready to move out in the morning."

"It's near morning now," I said.

Wes looked out the window. "We still got a couple of hours."

"I can't sleep," Lou said.

"You're on watch then," Wes said. "Unless someone else wants to volunteer, I'll take watch with her."

"I..." Was all I was able to say before Wes cut me off.

"Not you. We need you raring to go." He scanned the others. No one volunteered. "Me it is then." He started for the counter and then stopped. "Get on to sleeping already." Everyone but Lou moved to the back of the store.

I caught a glimpse of Lou and felt a strange feeling come over me. I didn't recognize it at first. It was like something gnawing away at my nerve endings. Suddenly I realized I was worried about her. I got Ajax's attention and called him to a corner of the store where we could be alone.

I spoke slowly as if he were an idiot. "I need you to do me a favor."

He nodded.

"Watch Lou."

He turned his massive head and watched her for a brief period and then turned back to me.

"No," I said. "I mean protect her."

He nodded enthusiastically.

"Don't tell her about this."

He shook his head.

"Good."

He grinned comically.

I patted him on the shoulder and relaxed as that gnawing feeling slowly disappeared.

***

I woke up the next morning with Kimball licking my face. I pushed him away and sat up, wiping the slobber from my cheek. The others were gone. I yawned and stood on unstable feet. I was weak. Maybe the time spent under the shunter's "care" was finally getting to me. I reached up to open the door and noticed for the first time that the room was smaller. There were no windows. The door was slotted. It folded open and shut. It was a closet. I pushed the door open.

I was in my parents' bedroom. I turned to look back in the closet for any signs of the convenience store. The floor was covered with clothes. Kimball was nowhere to be found. I heard a clicking outside the door of my parents' bedroom. This was all very familiar.

I placed my hand on the bedroom door knob, breathed deeply, and then slowly pulled the door open. I stuck my head past the jamb and peered down the hallway. I was about to breathe a sigh of relief when a man appeared at the end of the hall. With his gnarled fingers thrust forward, he stumbled toward me. A purple blob covered his face.

"Archie!" I yelled.

"Oz," a voice replied.

"Archie."

"Oz!"

The voice was coming from behind me. I turned toward it, and was horrified to see Gordy's dead Skinner sister staring back at me. I screamed and tripped over my feet as I attempted to flee. I fell to the floor face first with a thud. Woozy, I slowly rolled on my back and saw Lou looking down at me.

"Oz," she said quizzically. "You okay?"

I jerked up. "What..." I was no longer in my parents' bedroom. I was back in the convenience store. I hesitated and searched for an explanation. "Dream," I said. "It was just a dream."

Lou helped me to my feet. "I guess that means you were able to sleep."

"I guess," I said wiping my eyes.

"That's good," she said, handing me a Reese's Peanut Butter Cup. "Found a secret stash of candy in a filing cabinet in the manager's office."

I examined the candy. "Probably should give this to April or Ty..."

"There was enough for everybody," she said. "Eat it."

Relieved, I tore open the wrapper. I was starving. I devoured the candy. I wanted to cry it tasted so good. "Where are the others?" I asked with peanut butter stuck to the roof of my mouth.

"Out front waiting for us."

"Why did you let me sleep?"

"Even Creyshaws need their sleep, Oz."

I nodded. "I guess." I started for the door, but she stopped me.

"Are you mad at me?" she asked.

"No, why?"

She shrugged. "Kind of feels like you've been avoiding me."

"Nope," I said. We locked in a momentary stare. I could feel my heart begin to pound against my chest. I breathed in and marveled at how good she smelled.

"What?" she said.

Perplexed, I said, "What do you mean 'what'?"

"You're looking at me funny."

"I am?" I hadn't realized.

"Is there something you want to tell me?"

I shook my head. "Just that we should get moving."

She smiled and brushed past me. The touch of her gave me goose bumps. My one true love, I thought. That's crazy.

THREE

We spent the first half of our morning rummaging through a Walmart for supplies and a change of clothes. We all washed up with baby wipes. At Wes's insistence, April and Lou went to one end of the store with Kimball and cleaned up, while the rest of us went to the other.

"Lou is like my daughter," Wes explained. "I don't need to see her business. That ain't right."

"Yeah, well if it's all the same to you," Gordy said, "I'd just as soon not see your business either."

We each chose a separate aisle, undressed, and wiped ourselves down with the wet wipes. When we met back up in the middle of the store, we had new clothes and a clean baby smell.

"Now you people don't make me want to throw up," Gordy said.

"I wish I could say the same for you," Lou said.

"Ha ha," Gordy replied.

"Enough fun and games," Wes said. "We need some essentials. Everyone grab a backpack and fill it with a change of clothes, some bottled waters. Ajax and Ariabod, you two get to carry the food."

The gorillas nodded.

"Oz," Wes said, "we're going to need something to fight with. Come with me."

Everyone dispersed. Wes and I headed to the sporting goods section to gather up some weapons. Much to our delight, we found plenty of archery equipment, hunting knives, and camp axes. We were in business.

"Don't grab more than we need. It's best if we travel light," Wes said.

We gathered knives and axes for everyone, a couple of replacement crossbows, and plenty of arrows.

"We'll need flashlights, batteries, and rope, too," Wes said.

"On it," I said. I moved to the center walkway and looked for the sign for flashlights. I spotted it six aisles down and hurried to the aisle. I found six of the smallest flashlights in stock and turned to find the rope when I stopped dead in my tracks. A Taker stood at the end of the aisle. It chattered and sprawled its arms to the side. It was just a tad shorter than the shelves on either side of me. Slime dripped from its body.

"Easy, boy," Wes said from behind me.

I swallowed hard. "I'd forgotten how scary they are."

The Taker growled at the sound of my voice.

"It don't seem to like you much," Wes said.

"Misunderstandings are bound to happen. I did kill its queen after all."

The Taker opened its massive mouth and lurched forward. Thankfully it was too wide to enter the aisle way.

"I thought these things were overgrown pussycats now," I said.

"All bets are off since the Délons have lost control," Wes said. "We should assume that our friend here has bad intentions."

"That's not hard," I said.

"Back away slowly."

I did as instructed, and the Taker seemed confused by the narrow expanse of the aisle. It examined the shelves of goods on both sides. Placing one massive hand on the top of the shelves to its left, it began to rock them back and forth. The metal creaked and scraped as it began to give way to the Taker's strength.

"Quick step it," Wes said, a touch of panic in his voice.

"You said to back up slowly."

"Changed my mind..."

A thunderous pop echoed through the store as the Taker pushed the shelves over. I turned and ran to the other end of the aisle, zooming past Wes. The Taker bounded toward us, shaking the ground with each heavy footfall.

"Any ideas?' Wes yelled.

"Split up," I said.

"Not a chance..."

"This thing's after me, right?"

"So."

"So, he'll follow me wherever I go. You can get the others and take this sucker out before it eats me."

Wes hesitated. "Fine, but if you get ate before I get the others, I'm gonna be pissed."

"Hurry up then."

With that Wes broke off to the right and headed down an aisle that housed small kitchen appliances. I took the first left and pumped my legs as fast as they would go. As expected, the Taker pursued me and ignored Wes. I wanted to be relieved, but I couldn't really manage it. The Taker chattered and roared. I got the feeling it sensed that catching and eating me was just a matter of time. I hoped that it was going to be disappointed.

I rounded the next aisle to the right and stopped suddenly to prevent myself from running into an unexpected obstacle. I stumbled and fell to the floor. A hand reached down and helped me to my feet. Tyrone.

"Ty..."

He motioned for me to keep moving. "I got this." He pulled a hunting knife out of its sheath.

"C'mon," I said grabbing his arm.

He shook loose and ran in the direction of the Taker which by now was barreling down on us with more speed than I thought possible even for a mythical beast.

"Stop!" I said.

Tyrone dove across the floor and slid between the Taker's legs, slicing away at the monster's calves. The greasy beast screeched in pain and put on the brakes with such haste that it lost its balance and fell to the floor with a raucous thud. Ty was on his feet in a split second. He leapt on the Taker's back and started hacking away at it with his hunting knife. He was possessed. Mad.

The Taker was only momentarily disabled. It flinched and, in doing so, flung Tyrone from its back and stood. It was panting. It extended its claws and slashed a display of stuffed teddy bears. Tyrone scrambled backwards, trying to get to a distance where he could stand and mount another attack. The Taker stomped forward, slashing as he did. I was no longer its primary target. I reached in my backpack and pulled out a crossbow. I prayed I still had decent aim. I loaded it and quickly fired. The arrow lodge into the creature's lower back. It took no notice. In an instant, it wrapped its huge hands around Tyrone's waist and picked him up. The monster's mouth opened wide, and its jaws unhinged. Tyrone was about to be swallowed. I grabbed another arrow. My hands were shaky. I struggled to reload the crossbow. Hearing clicking behind me, I turned to see Kimball tearing across the polished concrete floor. He leapt through the air and buried his teeth into the Taker's backside. The creature roared and swirled around, knocking display items to the floor as it did. Tyrone fought to free himself from the monster's grip.

The Taker swatted at Kimball. The German Shepherd clamped

down harder. The creature let out a nerve rattling howl as it stumbled and crashed to its knees. Tyrone wriggled free and instead of running for safety, climbed on the monster's back. He raised the blade of the knife and brought it down with all his might into the back of the Taker's head. The monster let out a pained squeal and then went limp, collapsing on its barrel chest.

Tyrone screamed and repeatedly smacked the now dead creature in the back of the head. I approached slowly. I was more frightened of him than I had ever been of the Taker.

"Ty," I said quietly.

He continued to beat on the creature.

"Tyrone," I barked.

He turned to me, his entire body heavy. His teeth were clenched together so hard that I thought they might crack. His eyes were blood red.

"It's dead."

He looked at the Taker and then slowly climbed off its back, stumbling when his feet hit the floor. He somehow managed to keep himself from falling over. Just before walking away, he kicked the Taker in the ribs as hard as he could. "Not dead enough," he said. "Not dead enough." With that, he strolled past me and headed for the front of the store.

Wes approached from behind me.

I barely noticed him. I was focused on Tyrone.

"How'd you kill it?"

"I didn't. Tyrone did."

"Tyrone? Goodness knows. The boy's growing up."

I shook my head. "I'm worried about him."

"Worried? The kid just killed a thousand pound greasywhopper. You should be proud of him."

"You didn't see him. He was out of his mind."

"It's Valerie," I heard Lou say. I turned to see her standing next to Wes. There was a pained look on her face. I knew what she was thinking. It was her fault. Valerie was dead because of her. Because she trusted a Silencer. That Silencer killed Valerie. I knew that's what she was thinking because I was thinking it, too. I hated myself for it, but I couldn't help myself.

"He's going to have to get over it," I said. It was cold and uncaring. I didn't plan it that way, but it came out of my mouth that way. Wes and Lou looked horrified. Gordy and April had approached from the other side. They had heard me, but didn't react. "This is war!" I shouted. I'm not sure why. I wasn't mad. It was as if I wanted to make sure the entire world heard me. "People die in wars. People we know. People we love. People... we kill. We have to start accepting that. If we don't, there's no way we can win."

Wes cleared his throat. "This ain't war, son. This is survival. Dying kind of ruins that."

FOUR

Leaving the Walmart was harder than I expected. After we got over the shock of the encounter with the Taker, we settled in and gathered up as many supplies as we could find. The store was in pretty bad shape, but it was familiar

The truth was that little by little, day by day, you forget about your previous life. The first time you realize you can't remember a certain smell, or sound, or face as well as you used to, it bothers you. You'll give yourself a headache trying to recall it, but the really bad part is when you don't spend the time or effort to try and remember. It means you've totally given up without even realizing it.

The store was cold. I was cold. Numb really. I was back with my friends... my family. That's what they were, my family. I would die for them. I would kill for them. But at that moment, I felt like I was a million miles away. Something was not right. I should have been happy because I was back with them after being away for so long, but I wasn't. I drifted away from everyone else and found a corner in the stockroom where I could just sit and... not feel the others staring at me. It felt as though their eyes were always on me. Watching every move I made. I didn't know why exactly, but if I had to guess I'd say they were wondering if I was the same Oz that I was before I disappeared. I wasn't. Not by a long shot. But I wasn't sure if that was a bad thing or a good thing.

I settled in behind a pile of overturned boxes. They had been ripped open and emptied of their contents long ago. I took a deep breath and was surprised when I felt a lump form in my throat. I choked and coughed. Tears started to fall. I was crying. For no reason, or maybe for too many reasons to count. I fought to cry in silence. The more I did, the more it hurt. I needed to just break down and have an all out crying fit, but I couldn't let myself go. I could be discovered at any moment, and this wasn't the time to lose control. If they saw me crying, they'd be even more concerned about me. They wouldn't trust me, and I wouldn't blame them.

I thought I was past crying. I wasn't a kid anymore, not mentally. I was a warrior. "I am Creyshaw," I whispered in between sobs.

The word conjured up an image of Scoop-face in my mind's eye. Only I didn't picture him as Scoop-face. I saw him as Archie. The Délons had him. That was almost certain. The Myrmidons wouldn't be here otherwise. Those were the rules. Once a Storyteller is captured, their destroyer breaks through from... wherever it is they come from. The Myrmidons were little Bobby's Destroyers. They were his creation, and Archie was his warrior.

I looked up and gasped at the sight of April standing in front of me. I didn't know how long she had been standing there. I quickly hid my face and hoped she wouldn't realize I had been crying.

"What are we going to do?" she asked.

If she knew I had been crying, she didn't let on. "Settle in for the night," I said. "We'll hit the road in the morning."

"That's not what I mean," she said.

I studied her face. I had not really looked at her before. She was older than me, but the lost look in her eyes made her look years younger. "About what?"

"Bobby... Archie, they're still alive."

I sighed, brought my knees to my chest and wrapped my hands around my legs. "No way of knowing for sure." I knew in my heart that they were, but I wanted there to be doubt among the group to make my decision to go on without them easier. These are the tough decisions warriors have to make. That's what I told myself anyway.

"Yes there is," she said. "We should go back."

I was surprised by her assertion. I didn't know her well, but from what I did know about her I got the idea she wasn't the type to go all Marine on me and not leave a man behind. "Too risky."

"We can't just leave them."

"The Délons got Bobby. We know that because of the Myrmidons. If they got Bobby, that means..." I refused to go on.

"But you said they might not have been captured." she insisted.

"I was trying to be... optimistic." I stood. "It just doesn't make sense to go back."

"But Archie..."

"Stop," I said sharply. "Archie is either dead or... praying for death. Either way, we can't help him."

She started to shake. "I don't want to be the only one."

I furrowed my brow. I had no idea what she meant.

"They're gone."

I cleared my throat. "A lot of people are gone..."

"They're gone!" she screamed. "Tank, Bobby... Archie. I'm the only one left."

I understood. She had lost her family for the second time. I knew how that felt. I guess I should have told her that the fact that she survived meant she still had work to do, that she was destined to do something important, but I didn't believe it, and she would have heard the doubt in my voice. So I told her something I did believe. "You'll be gone soon enough."

She looked at me, horrified. "What do you mean?"

"I mean what I said. You're not going to be around much longer. None of us are." With that, I walked away but not before catching a disappointed look from Lou. She had been standing in the shadows listening to our conversation. I had a feeling she was sorry she had.

***

We dipped into bags of trail mix for dinner. The expiration date had come and gone long ago, but we were hungry enough to chance it. Beyond being a little chewier and stale, they were edible.

Tyrone ate with a faraway look in his eyes. No one really talked during the meal, but Tyrone somehow made his silence more noticeable than the rest of us. I caught a glimpse of his profile and was struck by how old he looked. Not older, but old. His complexion was gray, and he had huge bags under his eyes. Of course, I'm sure I did too, but I know they weren't as noticeable as his. He didn't just look tired. He looked like he was on death's doorstop.

Wes crumbled his empty bag of trail mix and tossed it aside. "That ain't gonna do for a big boy like me." He grabbed his extended stomach and shook it. "This belly is getting harder and harder to maintain."

Ajax grinned and nodded his massive head.

"How do you stay so fat?" Gordy asked without any malice.

Wes wasn't offended. He thought about the question and then said. "Don't know. Slow metabolism, I guess."

"It's because Stevie drew you that way," Lou said.

"Huh?" Wes said as he stood and stumbled over to the nearest overturned rack of snacks. It was slim pickings but he was determined to find something.

"That's the way Stevie drew you," Lou said. "Fat..." She gasped and cupped her hand over mouth. "Sorry."

Wes waved her off. "It's okay. Fat is fat. I ain't got nothing against it." He found a bag of peanuts and opened it with his teeth. "So I'm still fat because this is the way Stevie drew me?" He popped a couple of peanuts in his mouth. "How come you all are getting older? You're all 'bout a foot taller than when I first laid eyes on you... 'cept you, April. Don't know if anything's changed on you since all this began because we ain't known each other that long."

"I lost weight," she said proudly.

Wes sneered. "Good for you."

"I think it's all the Twinkies you eat," Gordy said. "I'm surprised that creamy filling doesn't ooze out of your ears."

Wes shrugged. "Can't help it if Twinkies keep for forever and a day. They's the only thing we find on a regular basis from over-turned store to over-turned store." As if the universe was trying to prove a point, he spotted a box of Twinkies near the stack of snacks he had just combed through. "You see!"

"Just because you find 'em, don't mean you gotta eat 'em," Gordy said.

"Son, food ain't something you pass up during end times," Wes said ripping open the box. He took out a Twinkie and tossed the box to Tyrone. "You better take one before I go through the whole box."

Tyrone handed the box to April without even considering taking one.

Wes stuffed then entire Twinkie in his mouth and shrugged. "You don't know what you're missing," he mumbled.

I felt a tap on my shoulder and turned to see Lou gesturing with her head for me to follow her. I stood and did as she requested.

"You need to talk to Tyrone," she said once we were outside

the building.

"About what?"

"Valerie," she said hesitantly.

I peered through the dirty glass door and got a glimpse of the group. Gordy, April, and Wes were deep in conversation while Tyrone stared off blankly.

"What can I do?" I asked.

"Help him deal with her... what happened," Lou said. "We need him, and he's useless to us if his head's not right."

"He'll work it out." I started to walk away, but she grabbed my arm and forcefully pulled me back.

"I don't get you," she snapped.

Normally her angry tone would have triggered an angry response from me, but for some reason, it didn't faze me. I honestly didn't care, and that bothered me. "It's not your job to get me, Lou."

"Job?" She looked hurt. "Why are you being such a jerk?"

"I'm not in the mood..." My plans were to storm off, but she stepped in front of me.

"Too bad for you because I want to know what's up with you... I heard what you said to April."

"I know."

"It was cruel."

"I know."

"You weren't like this before..."

"I disappeared? I know." I sighed. "I don't know what you want me to say. I'm a kid. I can't take responsibility for everyone else. If Tyrone doesn't get that people die in miserable ugly ways in this world then I can't help him. Same goes for April. It's not my fault they got Archie and Bobby. Archie is the same as me. He is Creyshaw. He had a job to do and he failed. I'm not going to go looking for him. I'm not!" My voice was getting louder and louder. "You want to know what happens if I find him?"

I could see real fear in her eyes as she backed away from me.

"I would have to kill him if he's not already dead!"

"What are saying?" she asked with a tear rolling down her cheek.

"The Délons have him. He will be marked, and he will be turned. You remember how they turn people, right?"

"I..."

I cut her off. The anger that had escaped me earlier was in full force now. "A shunter crawls out of its solifipod while you're sleeping and attaches itself to your face to suck out the part of your brain that makes you human."

"I don't understand."

"Because you weren't there. You didn't see what I did to him. I pulled the shunter off. I tore his face off. I can't do that to him again."

"Again?" She approached cautiously, reached out and gently took my hand. "None of this is real, Oz. You didn't do anything to Archie. I need you to see that. We don't belong in this world. The only way we can get back to where we belong is if we are all focused on getting home. We can't do this without Tyrone... or you."

I looked down at her hand holding mine and collapsed to one knee. "I'm tired."

She squeezed my hand. "That's allowed." She smiled.

I chuckled and looked up at her. "Wes is right. There's a chance that we'll never get home no matter how hard we fight."

She nodded. "Yeah, but there's a chance we will, too."

I stood and stared at her eyes. If I could, I would have never stopped looking at them, but a crashing sound in the parking lot diverted our attention. My body went stiff. Lou reached out and grabbed my arm. Her breathing was heavy and fast.

"What was that?" she asked.

I swallowed. "Wind..."

Another crash came, followed by the wap-wap-wap of feet on the ground. Wap-wap-wap. Wap-wap-wap. Lou and I backed toward the store entrance. Neither of us had any weapons. A conversation carried out in whispers drifted through the darkness.

"Not the wind," Lou said.

A cry, "Whoop!" sounded out from the back of the parking lot.

"Augh-wee-op!" was the reply. Whoever or whatever it was was just on the edge of the darkness.

"Whoop-whoo!" Another call.

I stepped forward.

"Where are you going?" Lou asked.

"Sounds like... a couple of kids," I said.

"Yeah, well the last bunch of kids we ran into tried to feed us to a bunch of locusts."

I turned to her and gave her point some thought. "Carl's group?"

She nodded.

"I remember. That's when you lost Tank."

"How did you know about Tank?"

Before I could answer, another call came from the darkness.

"What do you want?" I yelled.

I could hear the faint sound of whispering. They were bickering.

"Show yourself!" I yelled.

Nothing.

"You chicken?" I provoked.

The whispering got louder. Finally a single voice emerged. "We are the Throwaways!"

"Throwaways?" I mumbled. "You heard of 'em?" I asked

Lou.

"No," she said.

"What do you Throwaways want?"

There was a long pause. "We are the Throwaways!"

I chuckled and Lou shrugged her shoulders.

"You said that already," I answered.

There was another series of intense whispers and then the same single voice spoke. "We want... you to surrender."

FIVE

I saw the figure of a tall lanky boy hidden in the shadows. He held on to a staff. As he stepped closer, I could see that he was dressed too lightly for the chilly temperature. His face was thin and his skin was horrifically pale.

"Why do you want us to surrender?" I asked. "I didn't even know we were fighting."

"We are," the boy shouted. "We are the Throwaways. We are at war with everyone and everything."

"That doesn't sound fun," I yelled.

I heard the door to the store open and turned to see Ajax, Aribod, and Wes exit.

"What in the world is going on out here?" Wes asked.

"We've got visitors," I said.

"Who?"

"The Throwaways."

"We are the Throwaways," the boy said.

I shook my head. "They say that a lot."

"What do they want?"

"For us to surrender," Lou said.

Wes raised an eyebrow. "How many of them are there?"

"Best as I can tell," I said, "five, maybe a couple more."

Ajax hoot-growled and pounded his chest. Ariabod snorted like a bull.

"Hold on," I said. "I'm pretty sure they're harmless."

"Pretty sure ain't good enough," Wes said. "Lou, get inside and have Gordy, April, Kimball, and Tyrone sneak out the back and circle around behind these jokers."

"Whoa," I said. "I think we should just calm down. Let me talk to them."

"This world ain't really built for talking your way out of trouble," Wes said.

"Give me five minutes," I said. "Let me go out there and see if I can't talk some sense into them."

Wes thought over my request and then nodded. "Fine, but you're taking Ajax with you."

I winked at my old gorilla friend. "I wouldn't have it any other way."

Ajax and I moved ahead of the others. "We're coming out," I said.

"What for?" the boy asked.

"To talk about the terms of surrender," I said.

Ajax and I slowly made our way to the tall slender boy. I got a glimpse of two others crouched down nearby, behind a defunct street light.

The tall boy's face struck me as... incomplete. He had all the right parts, two eyes, a nose, a mouth. They just didn't have any... depth.

"What are your terms?" I asked.

"Terms?"

"Are we prisoners? Do we just get to leave? Maybe you want us to join your crew..."

"Can't join," he parked. "We are the..."

"The Throwaways. You said that about a billion times. I get it."

The tall boy pointed at Ajax. "He looks funny."

I furrowed my brow and snickered. "He's not exactly the kind you want to insult." I struggled to pinpoint what was missing from the tall boy's face. "What's your name?" I asked.

"I lost it," he said.

"You lost your name?"

He nodded.

I turned to look at Ajax for answers. He shook his head and grinned. I noticed his thick brow cast a shadow across his nose, and that's when it hit me. I turned back to the tall boy. No part of him cast a shadow.

"I have decided my terms," he said.

I was busy examining his face and nearly forgot what we had been discussing. "Oh, okay."

"We want to join your story."

The request surprised me. "Story?"

"We don't want to be Throwaways."

"What do you mean by story?"

He turned to his friends for guidance. They stood and approached cautiously. They were even less defined than he was. It almost appeared as if... part of them had been erased. In fact, one them had only half a right eye, and one arm appeared to be considerably shorter than the other.

The tall boy shrugged and said, "Story is just... life."

"Life?" I was starting to understand. "I accept your terms," I said.

The tall boy and his two friends smiled.

"How many Throwaways are there?"

"We are all Throwaways," he said confused.

"No, I mean how many will be joining our story? Is it just you three?"

He thought about the question. It was obvious he wasn't all there. He turned to the back parking lot and shouted. "Come forward. They have surrendered."

Three more of the strange looking Throwaways stepped forward... except for one. He or she... or at least half of a he or she was rolled forward in a cart by another with no face. There was just a flat blank surface where its eyes, nose, and mouth should be.

I was already beginning to regret the terms of surrender I had agreed to.

***

The Throwaways sat in silence near the first register in the Walmart. Kimball sniffed them when they first entered the store, but quickly lost interest. Ariabod didn't even acknowledge them. The front of the store was lit by a series of kerosene lanterns. The light did not do the Throwaways any favors. Their bizarre appearance was even more unsettling.

I offered them food. They hesitated as if they weren't sure they ate food. Finally, the Ttll boy took a bag of beef jerky from my outstretched hand. He smelled the bag. He knew enough not to eat the plastic, but he wasn't quite sure how to open it. I took it from him, ripped open the bag, and handed it back to him. He looked terrified as he pulled a piece of jerky out and examined it. Slowly, he brought the dried meat to his mouth and took a bite. There was a delayed reaction as he chewed. His face puckered and he swallowed. He smiled and turned to his friends. "Food." Those that had mouths followed his lead.

Gordy pulled me aside. "Excuse me, what exactly are these... things?"

"Throwaways," I said as if he should have figured that out on his own.

"If Throwaway means butt-ugly, then that makes sense," he said.

Wes joined us. "What are you planning on doing with these... fellas?"

I shrugged. "They said they wanted to be part of our story."

"What story?" Gordy asked rubbing his wounded shoulder.

"I knew it," Lou said joining our conversation. "We're back in the comic books."

"I don't think we ever left," I said.

"You lost me," Gordy said.

Wes waddled toward us. "Another comic book?"

April scampered toward us. "You guys, don't leave me alone with those things."

I looked over at the Throwaways. They were still amused by the prospect of eating. Even the one without a face. He... or she... or it rubbed a Frito up and down its featureless face. Tyrone sat a few feet from them and stared at them without a shred of emotion in his eyes.

"Stevie," Lou said ignoring April. "He had a lot of comic books."

"That doesn't make sense," I said.

"None of this makes sense," Gordy said.

"It makes perfect sense," Lou said, "or are you forgetting about Stevie's little Takers masterpiece?"

"No," I said. "But each Destroyer has its own Storyteller. They don't all come from Stevie."

"Kid," Wes said, "just cause Stevie had a bunch of comics don't mean he made 'em all."

I wanted to argue with him, but I couldn't. I'd gone through the comics in Stevie's room, but I didn't look to see if he had created them all. I was just looking for the one about the Takers.

Wes could tell his logic made sense to me. "I say we track our way back to Tullahoma. Get ourselves over to Stevie's house and find his comics."

April looked confused. "You guys are sure into comics."

"Don't look at me," Gordy said. "This whole conversation is about as geek-a-fied as it gets."

Lou grunted. "Try to pay attention, you two. The comics are... road maps. We can use them to find out what's going to happen before it happens."

"Just before," Wes said. "We can't forget about that. What if we find these comic books? Could be same rules apply. We read it and these... destroyer things will come after us."

I started to walk away. "They're going to come anyway."

***

I woke up several hours later to the sounds of Ajax and Ariabod grunting. They were sitting near the store entrance signing to each other. The conversation was intense. I feared that they may even start pounding on each other.

I found Lou sleeping nearby and nudged her awake. "I need your signing skills," I whispered.

She wiped her eyes and I almost felt guilty for waking her up. A good sleep was something that was few and far between in this world, and I hated taking that away from her, but then again this was a war.

She yawned and sat up. I pointed to the two gorillas. She looked at me and nodded as she climbed to her feet. "This better be good."

She moved closer quietly. "They're arguing," she whispered.

"No kidding," I whispered back.

"Ariabod doesn't like the Throwaways."

"They take a little getting used to," I said.

"Ajax doesn't like them either, but he..." she snickered. "The big dumb ape trusts you."

I smiled.

"They don't know where they came from."

"We'll figure it out," I said.

"No," she answered. "You don't understand. They're saying they don't belong." She watched the two gorillas sign back and forth. "Something about families. There is no family..." She groaned. "They're going too fast. They're saying something about family history."

"Family history?"

She studied the gorillas more intently, even taking a few steps forward. "The Throwaways aren't in the family history. That's what their saying. The Throwaways aren't part of the folklore. They don't belong."

I stood next to her. I looked at the gorillas with a suspicious glare.

"What's wrong?" Lou asked.

"If they know who doesn't belong, then that means they know who does. I wonder what else they're not telling us." I stormed off towards them.

"Oz," Lou said.

I ignored her and kept walking.

"Oz," she said louder. "Wait."

"They've been holding out on us," I said.

"Not Ajax," she said.

The gorillas heard us talking and hurriedly stopped signing.

"You don't want to make a scene," she said.

"No?" I answered. "I really think I do."

"Fine," she said stopping her pursuit of me. "Tell the two gigantic gorillas you're pissed off at them. That seems like a grand idea."

I stopped. Ajax and Ariabod flashed their teeth through a pair of grimaces. The size of them, their powerful builds, their dark eyes... approaching them with an attitude definitely was not a grand idea. I motioned for Lou to stand beside me. "How should I approach this?"

She shook her head. "You should let a woman handle it."

I bowed my head and gestured for her to go ahead.

She positioned herself in front of Ajax and Ariabod and asked, "How do you know they don't belong?"

They shared a look.

"You can't really whisper a sign," she said. "We saw what you were saying."

Ajax settled back on his haunches and signed. I moved in next to Lou and watched him effortlessly move from one sign to the next. Ariabod watched him steely eyed. Lou's eyes followed Ajax's hands.

"I don't..." she shook her head.

"What?" I asked.

"He's just repeating what we already know."

Ajax huffed and signed more frantically.

"They are... not nature..." She shook her head. "I think he means unnatural."

I snickered. "You think? Not much in this world is natural."

Lou continued to read Ajax's sign. "Gorillas always know...Gorillas don't know Throwaways."

I squatted. "Explain."

He signed.

"He just repeated himself."

I slapped his hand. "Come clean, Ajax."

He furrowed his thick brow and gritted his teeth.

Ariabod let out a muffled bark. Ajax gave him a reassuring look.

"What are you doing?" Lou asked concerned.

"Losing my patience."

"With a four hundred pound gorilla," she stressed.

"I don't care." I looked at Ajax. "Tell me what you know. Everything."

He signed.

"He said he... always talks... I think he means he tells you everything."

"Gorillas always know," I said. "You know everything. Everything includes how we can fix this thing. How we can bring everything back. Beat the Destroyers."

Ariabod excitedly signed.

Lou turned to me. "He thinks you're stupid. He thinks it's a waste of time talking to you."

"I'm not stupid. I'm mad," I said looking at Ariabod.

He motioned toward me and I flinched. Kimball appeared out of nowhere snarling at Ariabod.

"Everyone just needs to settle down," Lou said.

The tall boy emerged from behind the gorillas. "I understand," he said.

Startled, Ajax and Ariabod let out shrill hoots. The tall boy seemed almost amused by their reaction.

I stood. "I'm listening."

He leaned in and narrowed his eyes. "Is that how I should look when I'm listening?"

"What?" I groaned. "No, I mean tell me what you understand."

"I understand what they mean by gorillas always know."

I rolled my eyes. "And..."

"They mean gorillas always feel. They know because it feels as if it should be."

I peered around him to see if Ajax agreed with the tall boy. He nodded and grinned.

"Throwaways should not be," the tall boy said.

SIX

The plan was to go back to Stevie Dayton's house in Tullahoma. We were in a story. That had to be the answer. It made sense... as much as things could make sense in this crazy upside down world.

I wasn't looking forward to returning to Tullahoma. It was home. But it never could be again. Even if by some miracle we were able to bring the normal world back, Tullahoma would never be the same to me. I had watched it wither and die. I had seen it at its ugliest. I didn't know if I could ever shake those images from my head.

There was also the prospect of going back to Stevie Dayton's house. The last time I was there... Mrs. Dayton. They mutilated her, the Délons. Because of me. I drove her son to suicide. I destroyed her world long before it ended for the rest of us. But she still tried to help me. How could she do that? I had taken everything from her. Why didn't she hate me? The more I thought about how forgiving she seemed to be, the more I hated myself.

I was deep in a bout of self-hatred when I saw a Biltmore estate brochure appear in front of me. It took a second for my brain to register what I was looking at. I shifted my gaze from the brochure to the hand holding it. The meaty fingers and hairy knuckles told me immediately who the hand belonged to.

"We still going here?" Wes asked.

I took the brochure from him and examined the picture of the castle-like building. "What for?"

He shrugged. "It's a cool place."

"We don't have time to sightsee, Wes."

He snickered. "The way I see it, we don't know how much time we got. We got all kinds of monsters and bad guys chasing after us. We've been fighting and scraping and scrambling just to stay alive. We ain't had much to look forward to in a long time. Lou looked happy when we decided to go to the Biltmore. I don't think we should take that away from her... from everyone."

"But the comics..."

"Will still be there if we get there a day or two later... if they're there at all."

I looked at the others emerge from the Walmart and then back at the brochure. "Well, it is on the way."

Wes slapped me on the back and nearly knocked the breath out of me. "That a boy."

***

The wind cut right through us as we ascended the mountain interstate. If we had not stopped at the Walmart and both refueled and restocked our supplies, we probably would have needed to take a break long before we reached the exit to the Biltmore estate. Instead, we pushed through the conditions and kept going. Not without objections. As it turns out, April was very good at complaining. In a word, she was annoying. She even outshined Gordy in that particular skill.

I noticed as we walked that one of the Throwaways gradually positioned itself (it seemed genderless) closer and closer to April. It almost seemed to be studying her. Remarkably, it even started voicing the same complaints as April, although not quite as shrilly. In fact, its voice was monotone.

April didn't seem to mind. She was just glad to have someone who agreed with her.

They squawked and grumbled until we stood in front of the Biltmore. We all stood in silence and stared at the sprawling mansion. It was as beautiful as it was in the brochure, but there was something off about it. Of course, the lawn wasn't neatly manicured and the fountain was in poor condition. The walls of the mansion were faded and worn. We expected all of that. What we didn't expect was the feeling we got as we gathered on the cracked pavement of the driveway. We weren't wanted. None of us said it, but the alarmed look on everyone's face indicated we were all thinking the same thing. The mansion did not want visitors.

I cleared my throat. "Guys... ummm... I know this is going to sound crazy, but... I think we should just keep going."

Gordy shuddered. "The place gives me the willies. I'm with you."

Lou nodded. "Yeah... I've seen enough."

"Yeah, let's get going," Wes said.

We all turned to put the Biltmore far behind us as quickly as possible. But we stopped when we saw Kimball facing the exit with his hackles up and teeth bared. Ajax and Ariabod were nervously swaying next to him.

"That don't look good," Gordy said.

Tyrone stepped up. "There's somebody or something coming."

"How do you know?" Wes asked.

"You mean besides the animals freaking out? Thought I saw some shadows through the trees up there." He turned and looked back at the Biltmore. "In fact, it's going to be dark soon. I say we hole up in that mansion until morning."

"No," Wes said. He was as certain as I've ever heard him.

"My feet hurt," April added. "Let's just stay here for the night."

April's mimicking Throwaway repeated her suggestion.

Ajax raised up on his legs and pounded his chest. He and Ariabod were growing more and more agitated, as was Kimball.

Wes sighed. "Mansion it is, and I say we make it quick."

I called for Kimball, and we all sprinted to the mansion with Ajax and Ariabod bringing up the rear.

The mansion was a lot further away than we'd judged. We all arrived at the door winded, especially Wes. The rest of us thought he might have a heart attack. He wheezed and drooled and grabbed his chest. "No more Twinkies for me."

Lou gently placed her hand on his back. "You okay?"

He sucked in a deep gulp of air. "Fine... fine. I ain't dying if that's what you're thinking."

I noticed the other Throwaways for the first time since we took off for the Biltmore. I couldn't even recall where they were in the group as we ran toward the house. They stared blankly at the front door to the mansion.

"How about you, Tall Boy. You okay?" I asked.

He turned toward me. "Is that my name? Tall Boy?"

I thought about it and then shook my head. "Nah, we can come up with a better one." I pushed open the door to the mansion and peeked inside. A breeze swept past me. "We sure we want to do this?"

Kimball growled at the somebody or something we had just run from.

"Move," Tyrone said as he shoved me out of the way. He stepped inside the mansion and then turned back to us. "You coming?"

We followed two at a time.

Once inside, we stood in the large foyer and scanned the immediate area. The inside was even less inviting than the outside. The impossibly high ceilings were hidden under a layer of cobwebs and debris. Bug and rodent carcasses littered every corner I could see. The smell of mold and death filled the air. It was once a grand palace. Now it was an enormous tomb.

Gordy stepped beside me, his face buried in his sweatshirt. "Got a bad feeling about this, boss man."

"It's either this or whatever's outside."

He turned to the door. Ajax and Ariabod were still clearly agitated by whatever was out there. "Inside it is then."

"Yeah," I said. "But we stick together. No one goes anywhere alone in this place. We've got no idea if we're the only ones here."

Lou snickered. "I got a pretty good idea we're not."

We all remained huddled around the door for several minutes without saying another word.

Wes chuckled. "We've fought all kinds of big bad uglies, and we're afraid of a house. I say we find a table where we can gather round and eat like civilized people for once."

Still no one moved. I felt something brush past my leg. I looked down and watched Kimball slowly move out in front of the group. He turned to us and calmly woofed.

That was all it took for us to unglue ourselves from the foyer and venture into the mansion. It seemed to protest with each step we took. A musty breeze seeped through the cracks on the floors and walls. It almost seemed as if the Biltmore was breathing.

***

"This is the banquet hall," Lou said holding up the brochure. "At least, I think it is."

There was a large table in the middle with dozens of faded red cushioned chairs around it. The room was covered in the same thick layer of dust and cobwebs that was present throughout the foyer and hallway. There were three large fireplaces on the wall opposite the door. Two huge chandeliers swayed in the stale breeze.

"You could fit a football team 'round that table," Wes said.

"Sixty-four people," Lou said holding up the brochure again.

Wes did a quick head count. "Well, if you count Kimball, the go-rillas and... the new bunch of... Throw Outs..."

"Throwaways, dufus," Gordy laughed.

"Whatever," Wes said. "It adds up to 15 members in our party. You reckon the maître d' will seat us or do we gotta seat ourselves?"

April considered the question. "What are you talking about?"

"It's called a joke, little girl," Wes said. "Let's pony up to the table and have us a nice relaxed meal..."

A faint low rumbling sound traveled through the hallway behind us. A chill went shooting down my spine, and, by the looks on the others' faces, they were experiencing the same sensation.

"Wind," Tyrone said to himself as much as to any of us.

Wes chuckled nervously. "A relaxed meal may be too much to ask for, but let's give it the old college try."

We approached the table like we were all attached at the shoulders. The Throwaways appeared to be afraid only because we were. That is to say they weren't afraid at all. They were mirroring us.

We sat at the table and pulled power bars and nuts from our backpacks.

"Ration, people," I said. "The Walmart had been ransacked a couple of times before we got there. I got a feeling we're going to find fewer and fewer supplies from here on out."

They didn't argue, and I didn't watch over them like a hawk as they ate. I had issued my warning. It was up to them to listen to me or not.

As we ate, the mansion settled. Creaks, cracks, pops, and countless other noises seemed to sound off endlessly. Part of me thought the house was issuing a warning. It wanted us out.

I was in the middle of scaring myself by reliving every ghost story I had ever heard when Gordy nudged me. The subtle touch of his elbow on my arm startled me at first. I gave him a hateful glare.

"Dude," he whispered. "Look at no-face guy."

I complied with his request. The Throwaway with no face sat nearly motionless next to Tall Boy. "What about him?"

"You notice something different?"

I looked closely at No Face. He was on the other side of the large table, and the room was poorly lit, so I leaned forward. I scanned him up and down... and then I spotted it. There was a small bump in the center of his blank face. I squinted and zeroed in on the bump. "Was that there before?"

Gordy said, "No," without hesitation, and then he added, "I'm almost sure it wasn't."

I shook my head. "Probably was. Had to be. We just didn't notice it."

"He's changing," Gordy said. "Or she, or whatever it is."

I looked at him. "Into what?"

He shook his head slowly and said "What do we do?"

"We don't do anything," I said breaking off one last piece of my power bar. "Keep your on eye on... it."

He sneered. "Me?"

I smiled and nodded.

"C'mon, let someone else do it. What about April or Ty?"

"It's not like I'm asking you to marry it. Just watch it."

He growled. "But look at it. It's creepy."

"If it makes you feel any better, it probably feels the same way about you."

"He does not," Tall Boy said. He was sitting next to No Face.

Gordy and I squirmed. We had unintentionally gotten louder and louder as we talked. The Throwaways and everyone else in the room had heard us.

"He wishes for me to tell you he does not find you creepy, any of you."

I scowled at Gordy.

He smiled nervously. "Cool... Nothing personal. It's just the whole..." he waved his hand over his face. "I'm just used to... stuff being in this general facial area. Sorry."

With dinner out of the way, the question was what to do next. It was nighttime by now. Traveling in the daytime was dangerous enough. Doing it in the dead of night was insane. No one wanted to stay in the Biltmore, and it was fairly clear the enormous house didn't want us there either. We had to choose between an almost certain danger outside and what could be an imagined danger in the house. The house won.

"I say we go exploring," Lou said.

"What?" Gordy replied. "Are you nuts?"

"Yeah, I gotta say I don't see the sense in that at all, Lou," Wes added.

"I'd rather know what we're dealing with than sit around here and wait for something to come get us," she said.

"Waiting sounds good," April said. Her Throwaway mimic repeated what she said.

I gave the matter some thought. Finally I said, "I agree with Lou."

She smiled.

"Of course you do," Gordy said. "She's your girlfriend."

Lou looked terrified by his statement. I let out a sound that was either a laugh or a bark. Even I didn't know what to call it. "Shut up," I insisted.

"Whatever," he said. "I can tell you one thing, I'm not walking through this place by myself. You all are going with me."

"We'll go in threes," I said.

"Fine, I get the gorillas," Gordy said.

"You go with Ariabod and April," I said. "Ajax will go with Tyrone and Wes. Kimball is with me and Lou."

Gordy scowled at April. "Do me a favor and don't yap the whole time."

"Fine," she said. "As long as you aren't a stupid jerk-face the whole time."

"Oh, my God. I so hope you piss the gorilla off and he snaps you in half," Gordy groaned.

"Okay," I said. "April's with me. Lou, you go with Gordy."

She looked surprised, but didn't argue. She nodded and stood next to Gordy. April stuck her tongue out at him before moving next to me.

"Everyone happy now?" I asked.

"What about us?" Tall Boy asked.

"Oh," I said. I had almost forgotten about them. In fact, I realized that from the moment we first met it was very easy to forget that the Throwaways were there. "You guys should watch the front the door."

He scanned his group. None of them said a word, but they seemed to be having a conversation. He turned to me. "We feel that three is sufficient to watch the door. The rest of us would like to explore please."

I nodded. "Okay, fine. You pick who goes where."

"Me?"

"You're the leader, aren't you?"

He thought about the question. "Throwaways do not have leaders."

"Well, you do in this story. I dub you the leader of the Throwaways."

He smiled. "I will go with the fat man's group."

Wes rolled his eyes and shook his head. "Name's Wes."

The mimic huddled closer to April. "And I'm guessing she... I guess she's a she... she's going with us."

April tried to subtly put distance between her and the mimic, but it was pointless. The mimic matched her step for step. "Ewww," she finally said. "It's called personal space. Try it."

Gordy spoke up quickly, "Half-eye will go with us." He wanted to make sure he wasn't put in a group with No-face.

Lou shook her head. "We really have to give you guys names."

"Okay," Wes said. "We've grouped ourselves up. Who goes where?"

"How many floors are in this place anyway?" Gordy asked.

"Five, counting the basement," Lou said.

"Crap, there's a basement?" Wes said. "Never good in a place like this."

I nodded and sighed deeply. "We'll take the basement. Wes, you guys take the third and fourth floor. Lou..."

"Main floor and second," she said.

I nodded and smiled.

***

The basement was a maze of rooms and hallways. Kimball led our small group, and I brought up the rear. The mimic grabbed onto April's arm the second we started to descend the staircase. April was so scared she didn't care. In fact, she seemed to welcome it.

We passed down a long stone hallway and rounded a corner that took us to a room labeled with a brass name plate that read "Halloween Room." We paused. I closed my eyes and shook off the chill that was inching up my spine. "Go," I said to Kimball.

He did without looking back, traveling beyond the beam of the flashlight. April, Mimic, and I stood in the doorway. What we were waiting for, I don't know, but Kimball stepped back into the light and barked. I walked into the room, turned back to April and said, "Nothing to be afraid of."

"You're such a liar," she said. She grabbed Mimic's hand and took one cautious step inside.

I scanned the flashlight around the room. It was empty, and the walls were covered with a weird mural: a woman in a black veil, a fat friar or knight or something. It didn't help make the room fell less spooky.

We quickly made it to the other side of the room and entered a long narrow room. It took us a second to realize it was a two-lane bowling alley.

"Cool," April said.

"Yeah..." I was about to agree when I spotted something at the very edge of the light beam. I opened and closed my eyes to try to adjust them. It was a little girl in a black and white dress. She stood motionless. She was so still I thought I might be looking at another mural. I took a step. She didn't move. I turned to see if April saw her. The petrified look on her face told me she did. Of course, Mimic donned the same expression.

I continued walking toward the little girl. "Hello."

She darted back into the darkness.

"Let's go," April said. "Please."

I turned to argue, but had to suppress a gasp when I saw what was standing behind her. A snarling old man dressed in gray painters overalls stared at April with a... hunger in his eyes. I had no doubt he literally wanted to eat her.

"Step this way," I said restraining the panic that was building up inside of me. I tried desperately not to look shocked or horrified.

"Let's just go back," she said. Clearly, she had no idea what was behind her.

The old man took one lumbering step toward her.

"April," I said slightly louder. "Come here, now."

"No," she said.

The old man took another step.

Kimball growled and barked in his direction.

"Oh, that's nice," April said smugly. "You going to sic your dog on me?"

"He's not barking at you," I said.

She stiffened and finally caught on that I was staring over her shoulder. "What... what's behind me?" She swallowed. I could tell her mouth had gone dry.

"Never mind," I said. "Just walk this way, quickly!"

She took one step toward me when the old man reached out and grabbed her shoulder. She screamed bloody murder. Before I could move, Mimic hissed and shoved the old man, causing him to lose his grip on April. April barreled toward me wailing like a crazy person.

I moved my flashlight to illuminate her path. She nearly knocked me to the ground as she wrapped her arms around me, crying madly. I regained my balance and shined the light back to where Mimic and the old man were... They were gone.

"Let's go! Let's go! Let's go!" April pleaded.

"Where'd they go?"

She mustered up the courage to look in the direction I was pointing the flashlight. "She didn't follow me?"

Kimball started barking at something behind us. I turned to see the little girl standing in a doorway at the opposite side of the room. She smiled and motioned for us to follow her. I hesitated. We couldn't leave Mimic.

A low miserable moaning came from the Halloween room. The old man emerged from the room. Seething, he stomped toward us.

"Go, go, go," April said rapidly pounding my shoulder with the palm of her hand.

I thought about sending her on without me, but the old man scared the hell out of me. I couldn't explain it, but I was more terrified of him at that moment than I had been of anything we'd faced up to that point. He wasn't just menacing. It was as if he was hell itself. I didn't want to abandon Mimic, but there was no way I was going to confront the old man. I grabbed April's hand, and we ran toward the little girl. She had disappeared from the doorway, but that didn't matter. She was showing us the way out. I was sure we would see her again.

We bolted through the door with Kimball sprinting in front of us. We had entered a large room that was made up of a series of small dressing rooms. The old man was on our heels. I could hear him heaving and snorting. When I looked to see exactly where he was, I just saw a glimpse of shadows moving across dark corners.

We exited the dressing room area and stood in a smaller room. I quickly darted the flashlight beam from wall to wall. There was a small set of stairs leading up to another room. I pushed April in that direction and whistled for Kimball to follow. We dashed through the door. It was a room with an iron fence overlooking a hole.

"What is this place?" April asked breathing heavily.

"I don't know." Our voices echoed in the cavernous room. "Looks like an empty swimming pool."

A groan came from behind us.

"To the right," I said.

We nearly stumbled over each other as we erupted toward another door. Another short staircase took us up to a small hallway into a small gymnasium. Just as we were about to enter the room, the little girl appeared at the end of the hallway. She motioned for us to follow her. I grabbed April's arm and pulled her in that direction. "C'mon..."

An echoing scream crept toward us from the swimming pool below. April and I gasped in unison.

"Mimic," I said.

"Oh my God," April said placing her trembling hand over her mouth. "What are we going to do?" I could hear her struggling not to cry.

Mimic screamed again.

I pounded the wall with my fist. I wanted to block out her screams. She was just a Throwaway, after all. No one would blame us if we just left her. Not even the other Throwaways.

She screamed again. This time it sounded like she asked for help.

"You go. Take Kimball. Follow the girl." I said.

"No," April screeched. "I can't go alone."

"You won't be alone. Kimball will look out for you. He got me this far."

She grabbed my arm. "You can't go back there."

Mimic screamed.

"I can't leave her." I pried her fingers from my arm and tried to give her a reassuring smile, but there was no way I could pull it off. "Go."

She backed away slowly at first. The tears were flowing now. Kimball barked, and she took that as him telling her to hurry. She turned and did just that.

I watched her until she disappeared through the door. I was never sorrier to see someone leave. I pressed myself flat against the wall and took in a deep breath. After a count of three, I peeled myself from the wall and slowly went back the way I came. I don't know why, but I counted each step. On step twenty-three, I was back in the pool room. The air was different, cold and sickeningly sweet.

With a shaky hand, I held the flashlight in front of me. I

didn't want to see too much, so I kept it facing straight ahead, just enough to illuminate my path. I heard Mimic whimpering. I dashed down the path. I slowly turned to the right and saw what appeared to be a cross between a ladder and stairs leading down to the bottom of the empty pool. Before I took another step, I saw Mimic sitting on the surface of the neatly tiled pool floor. She looked different. I couldn't put my finger on it... yes I could. She was clearly a she. There was no mistaking it. In fact, she looked... like April. I shook my head. I was seeing things. The flashlight was getting weaker, and I was seeing things.

I slowly descended the ladder and stepped onto the pool floor. The soles of my shoes galumphed on the sloping surface.

"Mim..." I was about to call her Mimic even though that wasn't her name. "Are you okay?"

She turned to me and I saw her face for the first time. It was April. From the hair, to the clothes, to the way she looked at me, it was April. "How did you... I thought I told you to go with Kimball."

She just shook her head and whispered. "He's behind you."

I tensed up. My bones ached. The hairs on the back of my neck stood up. I felt movement just over my left shoulder. I swallowed and slowly turned toward it. He was there.

He was a small, thin man. His face was etched with sharp lines and covered in white and gray stubble. I was frozen in fear. His eyes were not vacant and dead, but sharp and cruel. He snarled and said, "Do you know Jeremiah?"

April or Mimic or whoever the girl was sitting in the empty pool grabbed my leg and pulled her body in next to me as close as she could. "Go away! Go away! Go away!" She pleaded.

The old man narrowed his gaze. "Jeremiah is my favorite!" Spittle flew from his mouth.

I reached down and forced Mimic-April to her feet. "We have

to get out of here."

The old man moved closer. "Do you know Jeremiah?"

"No," I barked. I wasn't angry. I was scared out of my mind. I could feel goose bumps forming on my arm. "I don't know who Jeremiah is."

"Grace knows Jeremiah," the old man responded.

"I don't know Grace or Jeremiah." I said.

"Nineteen nine," the old man said. "Jeremiah is my favorite."

"I..."

The old man looked past me. "You can't be here! This is mine!"

I was about to volunteer to leave when I realized he wasn't talking to me. I turned to see who he was talking to.

I was filled with relief and anxiety when I saw the dead that used to watch me sleep in the... facility. They were my connection to the Land of the Dead, and more importantly, they were distracting the old man. He stomped past us and headed for them in a huff. The dead backed away. The willowy boy in front looked as frightened as I felt.

I pulled Mimic-April to the ladder and quietly encouraged her to climb. She hesitated. I gritted my teeth and, slightly more animated, encouraged her to climb again. She finally did. I took one last look at the group of dead and the old man before I followed. The dead were slipping into the darkest end of the pool one at a time. The willowy boy gave me one last pleading look before being the last of them to disappear.

The old man turned his attention back to us and flashed a yellow-toothed grin. I scooted up the ladder without any further hesitation. In my haste, I dropped the flashlight and heard it crash to the ground.

"Go, go, go," I yelled.

Mimic-April clumsily climbed to the top and a split second

later I did as well. I could hear the old man clomping up the ladder. He was grunting like a madman. I grabbed Mimic-April's hand and pulled her toward the entrance to the pool. I decided to go back through the bowling alley and Halloween room. It was familiar and I knew that it would take me to the stairs. I was done with the basement and had no interest in ever seeing it again.

I navigated the dark corridors recklessly. Mimic-April and I crashed into walls and doors. The old man was having a much easier time of it. We heard him huff and puff as he pursued us, but there was no evidence that he was having trouble seeing in the dark like we were.

As we entered the bowling alley, I could swear I felt his cold breath on the back of my neck. I pumped my legs faster and practically dragged Mimic-April to the Halloween room.

As we raced through the room, I noticed an easing of the feeling of dread I'd felt since we first saw the old man. He was no longer chasing us. I could feel it. But, I didn't slow down and turn to verify my theory. I just ran and ran and ran.

***

We saw Gordy first. He approached wide-eyed when he saw our distressed faces. "You okay?'

I shook my head, struggling not to go into shock.

"What happened?"

I pointed down. "The basement," I said looking at Mimic-April in the better lighting of the main floor. She was not April. It was easy to see the difference. She was a faded copy of April. The coloring wasn't quite right. The facial features weren't quite complete. Mimic was a good imitation of April, but that's it. That's when it struck me. "Where's April?" I asked sounding panicked.

"Dude," Gordy said, "she's right there…" He stopped short

when he got a better look at Mimic. Stepping back in fear or disgust or both, he said, "What is that?"

"A Throwaway," I said. "She became April… kind of."

He clenched his jaw. "How?"

"I don't know," I said moving past him. "It's not important. Help me find April."

He hesitated, still fixated on Mimic-April. "I… I thought she was with you."

"We got separated."

"Separated?" he said.

I rolled my eyes as I grew frustrated having to explain everything to him. "There was… something in the basement. It chased us. We lost Mimic," I said gesturing to the incomplete version of April. "I went back to get her and sent April and Kimball in the other direction. I thought for sure that there was another set of stairs."

It was then that I heard the click, click, click of Kimball's nails on the floor as he sauntered toward us. I looked past him to see if April was following him. She wasn't. I almost asked Kimball where she was, and then I remembered he was a dog.

"You should see the winter gardens," I heard Lou say. "They're so beautiful... and creepy." She stopped short when she saw my face. "What's wrong?"

"April's missing," I said.

"She's right there," she said pointing at Mimic. I could hear her gasp after she took a closer look. "Wha..."

"Long story," I said. "Actually, I'm not really sure what the story is at all. I am sure that April is missing."

Lou shrugged. "Well, let's go find her."

I turned back toward the stairs. My mouth went dry. A chill raced through my body. "I can't..." I swallowed. "We can't go down there."

"What are you talking about?" Lou asked.

"Yeah, what's down there?" Gordy asked.

I shook my head.

"April's down there," Lou said.

I clenched my fist and thumped my leg trying to pound the courage back into my body. My teeth began to chatter.

"His name is Albert," Mimic said.

I turned to her astonished. "He talked to you?"

She looked at me dumbfounded. "He's Albert. He didn't have to say. He is the Flish."

"The Flish?" Lou asked no one in particular.

"A scary old man," I said.

Gordy laughed. "Old man? Dude, we've taken on purple dead-eyed freaks, ant men, zombie-things..."

"Takers," Lou added.

"Right," Gordy said. "You're sweating an old man?"

"He just looks like an old man," I said. "He's more than that. He's..."

"Evil," Mimic said.

Gordy waved his hand to illustrate his disgust. "Just do that thing where you get all strong and stuff. You know, from the marking."

I shook my head. "I don't like it when I get that way. It never feels like it will go away. And it only happens when I get mad. Not..." I hesitated.

"Not what?" Gordy asked.

"Scared," I said just above a whisper.

"I'll go," Lou said with a forced smile.

"No," I snapped. "No one goes. Not alone."

"Goes where?" Wes asked.

We all turned to see him, Tyrone, Ajax, and Tall Boy coming toward us.

"April's missing," Gordy said.

"Who's..." Wes began to ask looking at Mimic and then stopped. "What the..."

Tall Boy approached Mimic. "Did it hurt?"

Mimic nodded. "A little."

Wes cleared his throat. "I am all kind of confused. Someone want to explain to me what in tarnation is going on here?"

Gordy groaned. "April's downstairs somewhere. One of them Throwaways made herself look like April. And there's an old man in the basement who may or may not be a fish."

"Flish," Mimic said. "He is the Flish."

Tall Boy tensed up.

"That mean something to you?" Wes asked him.

"He is the Gray Man," Tall Boy answered as if we should all know who is talking about.

"Gray, pink, blue," Tyrone said pulling a hunting knife from its sheath, "what difference does it make?" He stomped toward the stairwell.

"Wait," I said.

A roar came from a back room. We all flinched and turned to see Ariabod dragging April's limp body out of the room.

Tyrone sprinted toward them. "Let her go, you dumb ape."

Ariabod snarled and refused to let go of April's arm.

Tyrone stomped his foot. "Haa! Get out of here!"

Lou jogged toward them. "What are you doing? He understands you. You don't have to act like a lunatic."

Ariabod smacked the floor with his free hand.

"If he understands me, why doesn't he let her go?"

She stepped in front of Ariabod. "Because you're not the boss." She smiled and calmly said. "You can let go of her."

He shook his giant head.

"Looks like you're not the boss either," Tyrone said. He turned to me. "Well?"

"What?"

"You're the boss man," he said. "Start acting like it."

I raised an eyebrow. I was getting tired of his act. If I hadn't been so relieved to see April, I would have let him know exactly how I felt. I sighed deeply and said. "Let her go, Ariabod."

The silverback huffed and gently released April's arm, letting it flop to the floor. Ariabod eyeballed Tyrone as he moved away, and Tyrone returned the favor. It was clear they didn't like each other.

Lou bent down and examined her. "She's alive," she said.

The rest of us formed a semicircle around them.

Wes peeked over Lou's shoulder. "Looks white as a ghost."

Lou felt her forehead. "She's cold." She stood and motioned to Wes. "Pick her up."

Wes did so without asking why.

"C'mon," Lou said walking quickly to the stairs. "There's a bedroom on the second floor."

"Bedroom?" Gordy said sounding incredulous. "What about the Flish? We need to get the hell out of here."

Lou didn't slow down. "April's in no shape to travel. We'll hide out on the second floor. What are you afraid of? It's all of us against him."

Everyone except Gordy and me started following her up the stairs. Gordy looked at me. "It's not enough, is it?"

I wanted to tell him it was, but he would have known I was lying. Instead, I just ignored his question and started up the stairs.

SEVEN

The fifteen of us fit comfortably in the bedroom that belonged to the original owner of the mansion. The furniture was an intense red and there was gold leafing on the walls. April was lying comfortably on the canopy bed with Kimball beside her. Lou and Mimic attended to her. The rest of the Throwaways assembled in the corner opposite the door to the bedroom. They mumbled to one another. I couldn't hear what they were saying, but I could tell they were deeply concerned. Wes was laid out on a chaise lounge in the middle of the room. Ajax and Ariabod huddled near him. Tyrone sat in a chair keeping a wary eye on the gorillas.

I stood by the window that looked out over the property and searched through the darkness for any signs of unwelcomed visitors. Gordy startled me when he spoke.

"We need to talk about our friends."

I pulled my head out from behind the red curtain and followed his gesture to the Throwaways. "What about them?"

He snorted. "One of them morphed into one of us, that's what about them."

I looked at Mimic hunched over the bed trying to get as close to April as she could. "Okay, it's weird," I said. "But not much isn't weird in this world."

"It's more than weird," Gordy said struggling to keep his voice down. "It could be dangerous."

"Dangerous?" I asked.

"What if they're like pod people sent here to take our place?"

"Pod people?" I laughed. "Have you met the Throwaways? They're about as gentle as you can get. Can't see them taking our place. They barely have their own place."

"Exactly," Gordy said excitedly. "They don't have a place here. They don't fit in. If they become us, suddenly they fit in."

I muddled through his logic quickly and then waved him off. "I think you're reading too much into this..."

"Am I? April goes missing, and Mimic winds up looking like her. In case you haven't noticed, No-face's bump is now a nose. I'm pretty sure the one with a messed up half arm now has a messed up two-thirds arm."

I looked past him and examined the group of Throwaways. No-face's bump did now appear to have nostrils. I returned my attention to the world outside the window. "We'll keep our eye on it."

I could almost hear him grinding his teeth together in frustration at my lack of concern. "You suck as leader."

I didn't turn to him immediately. I felt an anger building up inside of me that would have led me down a path I didn't want to take. The painful ice cold blood of my Délon marking started to course through my veins. I sucked air in and held my breath until I felt the rage start to subside. Still, I didn't acknowledge him. I waited and waited until the feeling was completely gone. If he had pushed the argument, I probably wouldn't have been able to control it, but thankfully, he remained silent. Maybe he sensed what was bubbling up inside of me and wisely decided to back down.

I spoke calmly and slowly. "I didn't ask to be leader, numbnuts. I don't know what the hell I'm doing. Since I've got no experience with this kind of thing, I'm going with my gut, and my gut tells me that the Throwaways aren't dangerous. In fact, my gut tells me we could use them."

He bit his lip and actually thought before he spoke, something he didn't do a lot of. "How can we use them?"

I shrugged. "I'll let you know when I know."

He threw his arms up in disgust. "Fine. But I'm watching them like a hawk, and I'm not going to be nice about it."

"Your choice," I said. I was about to look out the window again when I caught a glimpse of Tyrone's face. He was glaring at Ariabod. He squeezed and released the handle of his knife over and over again. "I think we need to worry about Tyrone more than the Throwaways."

Gordy looked over his shoulder at Tyrone. "Kid's messed up. Lou says he was really gaga over Valerie. He ain't been the same since she got killed."

"He's going to wind up doing something stupid," I said. "Get himself killed and who knows who else."

"What do you want to do?" Gordy asked.

I shook my head. "Nothing for now, but while you're keeping an eye on the Throwaways, keep another on him."

Gordy chuckled. "Safer watching the freaks. I'm pretty sure I can take them. That kid's had his heart broke and ripped out of his chest. He ain't got nothing to lose. He's liable to go nutbag crazy and kill me just for looking at him funny."

"Then try not to look at him funny," I said walking away and heading for the bed.

"You're a real big help," Gordy said.

"How's she doing?" I asked Lou as I approached the bed.

"She's warmed up a little. Her temperature's almost normal I think. Can't tell for sure without a thermometer. She's still a little delirious. Mumbling about the old man and someone named Grace."

"Grace?" I said looking at Mimic.

"You know the name?" Lou asked.

"The old man said something about Grace." In my head, I replayed every word he'd said down in the pool. "Jeremiah... Did she say anything about someone named Jeremiah?"

"No," Lou said.

"Nineteen nine," Mimic added.

"What?" Lou asked.

I thought for a minute. "Yeah, that's right. He said something about nineteen nine."

"Jeremiah nineteen nine," Mimic said without taking her eyes off April.

"Nineteen nine?" Lou sat on the edge of the bed. "Code?"

"Don't know," I said. "Sounded just like rambling to me."

Lou folded her arms and stared intensely at the canopy on the bed. "Jeremiah, Grace, nineteen nine."

I sat on the bed next to her. I got a faint whiff of her sweet scent and momentarily lost my place in time. I zeroed in on her neck. I had never noticed how… pretty it was. The thoughts running through my head started to make me feel uneasy. I cleared my throat in an effort to shake them loose and shouted, "He said Jeremiah was his favorite."

She jumped at the volume of my voice. "Oh… okay..."

"Jeremiah?" Wes barked from his lounge chair. "From the Bible?"

I twisted my head around. His hands were behind his head. He looked far too relaxed for a guy trying to survive the end of the world. "The Bible?"

"Yeah, the Bible. It's a book. You heard of it?"

I nodded absentmindedly. "Why would you think we were talking about the Bible?"

"It's the only Jeremiah I know," he said. "Old testament. A

lot of death and destruction, if I remember right."

Lou and I looked at each other. We both said, "Nineteen nine" at the same time.

"It's a verse," she said.

"From the Book of Jeremiah," I added.

She jumped up and scanned the room. Spotting a dresser nearby, she ran to it as quickly as she could. She frantically started going through the drawers.

"What are you doing?" I asked.

"Looking for a Bible. There's got to be one here…" She giggled as she reached in and pulled out a black leather Bible. "I knew it!" She flipped through the book, stopped, turned a few more pages, and ran her finger up and down a page. "19:9," she repeated to herself a few times. "Ahhh! Got it!" She read silently. Her eyes narrowed. I could tell she was reading the verse a few times.

"What does it say?" I asked.

She looked up and simply shook her head as if to say she couldn't bring herself to read it out loud. Before I could stand, Gordy moved in and yanked the Bible from her hand. He sighed and found the verse. He didn't bother reading silently to himself first. He just blurted out horrible word after horrible word as loudly as he could.

"And I will cause them to eat the flesh of their sons and the flesh of their daughters, and they shall eat every one the flesh of his friend in the siege and straitness, wherewith their enemies, and they that seek their lives, shall straiten them. " He peered up over the leather bound book. "Whoa!"

Every face in the room, even the blank one, froze.

"So, there is a dude in the basement who's into eating… people?" Gordy asked. "Why exactly did we decide to stay here?"

"Is he Skinner Dead?" Wes asked. The relaxed posture was

gone. He was sitting up and rubbing his stubbly chin with his callused fingers.

"No," I said.

"Was he real… you know, alive?" Lou asked.

"I don't know…" I stood and stared at the floor as I tried to remember every detail of the old man. "The boy..." I said.

"What boy?" Wes asked.

"The dead boy, the one from before. The one that wanted us to follow him to the Land of the Dead, he and the others were there… in the basement. The old man wasn't too happy to see him."

"Others? What others?" Lou asked.

"The other dead."

Gordy threw up his arms. "Great! We're in a creepy old mansion with a bunch of dead people in the basement and one scary old dude who wants to eat us. This just gets better and better!"

"Boy," Wes barked, "you're 'bout to get a good dose of my foot up your keister. " He lifted himself off the chaise lounge and was almost winded by the effort. "What are the chances we just stumbled on the place they wanted us to go?"

"Slim to none," I said.

"That brochure about this place you found at the convenience store, how'd you come across it?"

I thought about it. "The wind... It just caught my eye."

He rubbed the back of his neck and shook his head. "That weren't no wind. Dollars to donuts it was one of your dead friends giving us a nudge in the right direction."

"Well," Gordy said. "They got us here, let's just call them upstairs and get this thing over with."

"How do you propose we do that?" Wes asked.

Gordy shrugged. "I don't know, séance maybe?"

Wes hesitated and then smiled. "That just might work."

April let out a deafening scream. She sat up straight in bed and started bawling. "Mommy," she cried.

Mimic hastily backed away. She shrieked like an injured animal.

Lou ran to April's side. She began by encouraging April to lie down and then resorted to physically trying to force her.

"I kissed him on the cheek," April cried hysterically. "That's when he decided to eat me."

While Lou wrestled with her, the rest of us stood frozen in time and listened to her horrific story.

"Mommy let me go to a party with him. I picked wild flowers outside while he sharpened his knives in the kitchen. He called me inside and grabbed me. I told him I would tell mommy that he was a mean man. "

Tyrone held tight onto his knife handle. "Tell her to shut up," he demanded.

"He choked me. I kicked and screamed and scratched."

"Shut her up!" Tyrone pleaded this time.

"It took him nine days to eat me."

Tyrone raised the knife and repeatedly stabbed the vacant side of the bed. "Shut up! Shut up! Shut Up!"

The Throwaways huddled closer and closer together until they were almost one jumbled mass.

April sucked in a long breath of air and then collapsed into a blubbering mess.

I had had enough of Tyrone's act. Without considering the consequences, I barreled into him and knocked him to the floor. Thankfully, the knife went flying out of his hand. I raised my fist, prepared to pummel him within an inch of his life, when I saw the expression on his face. It was calm. He wasn't fighting back. He wasn't screaming or thrashing about. He was waiting for me to hit him. I let him go and stood up.

"What is going on here?" Lou asked sounding as stressed as I felt. She had an arm draped over April's shoulder.

"This is crazy town," Gordy added. "The heart of it!"

My hands began to shake. "It's this room," I whispered.

"Speak up," Wes demanded.

"The room feels different," I said.

Wes looked around and then crossed his arms. "Got colder, that's for damn sure."

Tyrone found his knife and picked it up. "He's here."

I shook my head. "No. It doesn't feel like him." I spun around to face Tyrone and in doing so happened to glance at the dark corner of the room. There, almost blending in with the black shadows stood the little girl from the basement. My heart raced. I tried to tell the others, but I couldn't speak.

"It took him nine days," she said. At least I think she did. I saw her lips move, and I heard her voice, but no one else reacted. "Nine days," she said just before she vanished into the darkness. The coldness was gone.

My legs began to wobble, and I struggled to keep my feet. I bent over and placed my hands on my knees, breathing deeply.

"What's wrong with you, son?" Wes asked.

"We've got nine days." I straightened up, shivered, and rubbed my hands together.

"For what?" Tyrone asked. He was stoic and detached.

"I'm not sure," I answered.

"Nine days?" Gordy yelped. "I'm not particularly interested in sticking around here for another nine minutes. I say we get on our giddy up and put some serious miles between us and this freakfest."

"Can't," I said.

"Oh man!" Gordy stomped his foot. "No one ever listens to me!"

"Because you're a moron," April said.

None of us noticed that she had spoken at first. Her voice was weak, but it was actually April speaking this time, not whatever it had been before. As if we were all connected to the same thought, everyone in the room did a delayed double take.

Lou rubbed her back. "Are you okay?"

April weakly shook her head. "No, not even close." She winced. "I feel like my insides have been shredded."

Mimic giggled. She brought her hands to her face and swayed back and forth. She was clearly happy to see April back to her old self… almost.

April turned to the Throwaway and recoiled. "What… June?"

Mimic smiled softly. "Does it please you?"

April scooted across the bed to get away from Mimic.

"June?" I looked to Lou to see if the name meant anything to her. She looked as confused as I was.

"No," April said staring dumfounded at Mimic. "That's impossible."

"It is what you wanted," Mimic said.

April was too shocked to respond.

"Who's June?" I asked.

Mimic looked at me and smiled. "I am."

"No!" April barked. "No, no, no!"

"April," Lou said loudly, but gently. "Calm down. It's okay."

April looked at her in irritated awe. "Don't tell me it's okay. Don't tell me that." She pointed at Mimic and screamed. "You are dead... June is dead... My sister is dead!" She buried her face in the pillow and started to wail.

EIGHT

April cried herself to sleep. The rest of us tried to collect ourselves. We were all on pins and needles. All of us except the Throwaways. They were eerily calm. Even Mimic. We had to pry her away from April's bedside. She told us several times that she needed to stay by her sister's side, but at my prodding Tall Boy talked to her and convinced her to join the other Throwaways.

The questions came fast and furious among us non-Throwaways. First, Wes wanted me to explain what I meant when I said we had only nine days. I had to tell him on several occasions that I didn't know. For some reason, he felt that if he asked me the question in a slightly different way over and over again, I would finally be able to give him the answer he wanted. All it really accomplished was making me more and more irritated with him and making him more and more frustrated with me.

We were at each other's throats. Something was under our skin and I had a feeling it had very little to do with us.

Wes shook his head. "Let's just settle down a bit here and go over what we know."

"We know it don't make a lick of sense to stick around here," Gordy said.

"Stop your grousing," Wes said. "It ain't helping."

Lou took a deep breath and composed herself. She was in better control of her emotions than the rest of us. "We know it took him... whoever he is... nine days to eat her... whoever she is."

"He is Albert," I said. "The Flish, and she is Grace."

Wes looked puzzled. "Albert... the Flish and Grace. Why is that familiar?"

"Must be an old guy thing because it doesn't mean a thing to me," Gordy said.

I looked at Ajax. "What do you know?"

He sat back on his haunches and grunted. Nothing.

I shifted my gaze to Ariabod. "You?"

He signed and Lou interpreted. "Fish gets in."

"What do you mean by that?"

Lou watched him sign again. "He said he means what he said."

Ajax joined the conversation with some signing of his own.

Lou hesitated before she interpreted. "Ajax says he means fish haunts from within." She added her own interpretation. "I think they're saying the Flish possesses people."

"Possess?" Gordy asked. "Like in the movies when a ghost takes over a person."

"Not a ghost," Lou said.

Gordy waited for Lou to expound on her statement, but she remained silent. He sighed and shook his head. "What is it if it isn't a ghost?"

She still hesitated.

"Answer him," I insisted.

She readied herself and said, "The devil."

There was a burst of silence. That's the only way to describe it. It practically blasted the room apart.

"The devil," Gordy finally said. "Evil guy? Horns? Pitch fork? That's what you're saying, right?"

She shook her head. "I'm not saying it. Ariabod is."

"No," Gordy snapped. "He said the fish gets in. You took

that and brought the devil into it."

She began to lose her cool. She gritted her teeth and said, "I'm just trying to make sense of all this, that's all."

"Okay," I said. "This isn't working. We can't keep jumping down each others' throats."

Wes chuckled. "That's easier said than done, Oz. I'll be honest with you, I got a knot in my gut that is irksome as hell."

I nodded. "Me too."

Lou grimaced. "No knot, but you all are definitely irritating me."

Gordy shrugged. "Not sure what irksome means, but like my old man used to say, I feel like I'm wired for a fight."

"So what do we do?" Lou asked.

"Wait it out," Wes said.

Gordy groaned. "In the house?"

"Just for the night. We'll head out in the morning..."

"No," I said.

"No?" Wes replied.

"You're forgetting the Land of the Dead." I avoided eye contact with any of them.

"The Land of the Dead?" Gordy said. "You've got to be kidding? Who gives a flip about the Land of the Dead?"

"We were led here..." I started but Wes cut me off.

"The little piss-ant's got a point. We should stick to the Tullahoma plan. Let's get back there and find them comic books. I thought you said the answers was there?"

"They are... well, I'm pretty sure they are, but that doesn't mean we can forget about everything else. They want us to go to the Land of the Dead. We have to go."

"Who is they?" Wes asked.

I shrugged. "I don't know exactly, but they've been trying to get my attention for a long time." I thought back to my time in the "facility" when they watched me sleep.

"Can we vote on this?" Gordy asked.

"No," I said moving away from Wes and positioning myself closer to Lou. The pain in my gut eased. I stepped away from her and it got worse. I stepped back toward her, and the pain was gone. I quickly walked to Gordy. The pain intensified. I stood next to Wes. The same thing.

"What the hell you doing, boy?" Wes asked.

"It's us," I said.

"What's us?"

"The knot... the thing that's got us all on edge. It's not this room or this house. It's us." I couldn't explain why I didn't get the feeling from Lou, but I definitely got it from the others. I suspected she would put the knot in my stomach soon enough.

Tyrone chimed in for the first time and his tone was so unnaturally calm it was unsettling. "He's already inside us."

I swallowed and whispered, "We have nine days."

"What happens after nine days?" April asked.

Wes answered by repeating part of Jeremiah 19:9, "And I will cause them to eat the flesh of their sons and the flesh of their daughters, and they shall eat every one the flesh of his friend in the siege."

The burst of silence was back.

"He can't make us... I mean we wouldn't... I wouldn't..." Lou couldn't say it no matter how hard she tried.

Tyrone stared blankly. "That's what the knot is, hunger."

Gordy nervously cleared his throat and spoke in a squeaky voice. "If y'all want me to stop freaking out, you gotta stop telling me this stuff."

"Relax," I said.

"Relax?" Gordy roared. "Wes is already looking at me like a Twinkie."

"Boy, I'm going to punch your teeth down your throat!" Wes said stepping toward him.

I got in the middle of them and shouted, "Enough!"

Everyone in the room worked to calm themselves.

"We have to separate," I said.

"Separate?" Gordy said. "We have to leave."

I shook my head. "Leaving won't do any good. This thing will go with us."

"You don't know that," Gordy laughed a little too loudly. "You don't know anything."

I fought to keep my emotions in check. "I know that the dead brought us here. We have to... I have to go to the Land of the Dead. Don't ask me why because I don't have an answer for you."

Lou looked at me concerned. "I don't think we should separate. What if something happens?"

"Something is going to happen if we stay together," I said.

Wes breathed in deeply through his nostrils and stood tall. "Oz is right. We need to split up. We got enough two-ways to go around. We'll keep in touch for as long as we can." He looked at the Throwaways. "They don't seem to be affected."

I turned to them. They clearly weren't at each other's throats. "Then we won't be alone at least. There are six of us and six of them. We'll each take one."

"Won't we... eat them?" Gordy asked. He was even shocked by the words that had come out of his mouth.

"No," I said. "I think they're safe because they're not... human."

"Are we really saying this," Lou asked. "You think he can make us eat..." She didn't finish.

"I do," I said as coldly and flatly as I could. I wanted her to understand that I wasn't willing to consider any other possibilities.

We needed to take action now, and it wasn't open for debate.

She got the hint asking, "What about April?"

I grumbled because I had forgotten about April, and I was angry with Lou for reminding me. "You stay with her until she can take care of herself."

Gordy laughed. "That'll be never."

"It'll be by tomorrow," I said. "Has to be." To Lou, "I want you to put some distance between you and her in the morning. We've got no idea how this thing is going to go down. Explain it to her when she wakes up. Don't let her talk you into staying. Mimic or June or whatever her name is should stay with April."

Wes had retrieved all the walkie-talkies and handed them out.

"But she hates Mimic," Lou said.

I nodded. "True, but Mimic seems pretty devoted to her. She'll look after her." I took the radio from Wes and turned it on to test it.

Gordy tapped me on the shoulder. "You're forgetting something." He pointed at Ajax and Ariabod. "Are they going to eat us?"

Ajax furrowed his brow and shook his massive head.

"There's your answer," I said.

"One of them goes with me," Gordy said.

"Hold your water," Wes said. "They go with the girls."

"I can take care of myself," Lou snarled.

"Ariabod goes with April," I said.

"And Ajax?" Lou asked.

I hesitated because I knew she wouldn't like my answer. "He goes with you."

"I said I can take care of myself!" She said.

"I know you can, but you're the only who can do the sign language thing. Might as well take advantage of that." I smiled proudly. It was a plausible excuse, and that was a small part of the reason I wanted Ajax to go with her. The bigger part was I couldn't stand the thought of her getting hurt or... killed. Ajax would look out for her just as I'd asked him to do at the convenience store.

I grabbed my pack and was headed toward the Throwaways to tell them the plan when I heard a woof. Kimball tilted his head and studied me. I managed a smile. "You're with me."

He barked.

DAY 1

NINE

I wanted to get as far away from the basement as possible, so I went up to the fourth floor. Tall Boy was my Throwaway companion. I didn't pick him. He picked me. All the Throwaways made their own choice as to who they would pair up with. I didn't mind Tall Boy's company. I just wished he would talk more. It was a little unsettling to be with someone who only spoke when spoken to. I guess I was too used to Gordy spouting off about this and that nonstop.

We investigated the entire floor before settling on the Observatory as our base of operations. It was a two story room with a spiral staircase that led to a rooftop access. For some reason, I felt safe knowing that the room had an exit, even though that exit brought me face to face with gargoyle statues and the like. They were preferable to meeting up with the Flish.

I sat on a large chair and mulled over our current predicament. Away from the others, I felt like I could breathe again. The knot in my stomach was a distant memory. I was convinced that we made the right decision by splitting up. That's not to say I was happy being apart from the others. I had had my fill of being without them. All that time spent in the facility made me realize that they were more than just a group of people I had survived the end of the world with. They were my new family. Having lost my first family, I wasn't wild about the prospect of having to ditch Lou and the others.

Lou.

Her name bouncing around in my head was enough to make me insane with worry. I worried about the others, too, but not like I worried about Lou. I got a pain in my chest every time I imagined something terrible happening to her and, in this world, it was impossible not to think something horrible would happen to her.

I sighed and tried to push all thoughts of the others out of my head.

I heard Tall Boy sigh. I shook my head. "Don't do that."

"Do what?" he asked.

"That thing Mimic did with April."

"What did she do?"

I rolled my eyes. "The mimic thing. She basically became April."

"She did not," Tall Boy answered. "She became June."

I conceded his point. "Well, don't do that then."

He looked at me puzzled. "Of course not, June is already here."

I snickered. "Well, she's really just June-like, isn't she?"

He thought about my question. "I don't understand."

"June… she's real or she was real. Mimic just made herself look and sound like her."

He still looked confused. "I don't understand this 'real'"

I struggled to find a good definition for him. "It means… actual. Something that really exists."

"Exists?"

"Something you can touch and feel."

He shrugged. "I can feel June."

I groaned out of frustration. "Yeah, but she wasn't meant to… be here."

"She's not here."

I shook my head and unintentionally raised my voice. "No, I don't mean here." I illustrated my point by waving my arms in a circle. "I mean here, in this world."

"What world does she belong in?"

I considered his question carefully. In trying to explain to him what 'real' meant, I was becoming more and more confused about the meaning myself. The fact was this was the perfect world for June. "I'm not explaining this right because we're in a world that's not real right now."

He smiled faintly. "I think real is not so complicated. If a thing is, it is real."

I smiled back. "Someone smarter than me could tell you exactly why you're wrong, but since they're not here, let's just say you're right."

His smiled broadened.

"That doesn't mean I want you to do what she did."

"That is up to you."

I raised an eyebrow. "Meaning?"

"Throwaways do not have a say in who they become. April made June."

"How?"

He shook his head. "I have never become, so I don't know. June only said that she felt a thought from April."

"Felt a thought?"

"A void, as if something that should be wasn't. For April, June should be."

I searched my mind for a thought, something I could feel. There were too many to choose from, so I took a deep breath and attempted to push every thought out of my mind.

I peered over at the opposite corner of the room and admired the spiral staircase. It led up to a wrought iron balcony. Shadows danced and swayed on the walls. The motion relaxed me. It should have unnerved me, but for some reason I found it soothing. I felt my eyelids get heavier and heavier until I couldn't keep them open any longer. Just before I closed them I said, "If I fall asleep, you're in charge."

Tall Boy didn't answer.

"Hear me?" I asked.

He still didn't answer.

I turned to him. He stared at me with a half-smile on his face. "Did you hear me?"

"I did," he said. "I thought you were talking to Kimball."

Kimball's ears perked up at the mention of his name.

I chuckled. "You've got self-esteem issues, my friend." I closed my eyes. "I was talking to you."

"How do I be in charge?"

"Just sit there and wake me up if you hear anything..." I was asleep before he could ask another question.

***

I dreamed of Anthony and the day we both died. We were caught in the current and struggling to keep our heads above water. An invisible tide of water wrapped around my ankles and tugged me beneath the surface. I swallowed the salty water. I jerked and fought to release myself from the grip of the ocean. I peered through the murky water and saw Anthony. He was terrified. As hard as I struggled, he struggled twice as hard. I reached for him. Maybe together we could fight our way out of the current. A hand grabbed onto my wrist and pulled me away from Anthony. I watched as he grew smaller and smaller. A face appeared in the blue and green water beneath him. It was the boy from the Land of the Dead. He gently latched onto Anthony's foot and pulled him down.

***

"I hear anything," Tall Boy said.

I stirred out of my dream and opened one eye. "What?"

"I am waking you because I hear anything," he said.

I processed the information and then sat up with a jolt. "What... What do you hear?"

Just as I asked, I heard a creaking as if someone or something was stepping on a loose floorboard. I stood. The scruff of Kimball's neck was on end. "Who's there?"

We heard the creaking again. It was coming from above us. Someone was on the roof.

Kimball woofed.

I located my crossbow and armed it.

"What do we do?" Tall Boy asked.

"We either wait for them to come to us or we go to them," I answered.

Kimball barked.

"I was afraid you were going to say that," I said.

Tall Boy looked amused. "Did he say something?"

I nodded. "Plain as day."

"What?"

"He says we should go to them."

Tall Boy looked even more amused. "Is he always right?"

I smiled. "So far." I moved to the staircase. Tall Boy started to follow. I motioned for him to stay back. "You be the fall back position." I spotted a floor lamp. "Grab that lamp and if anything other than me comes down those stairs you knock the crap out of it, and then run like hell to warn the others."

He nodded.

I looked at Kimball. "You help him."

He sat and looked up at the roof access.

I started my climb up the spiral staircase. It was a narrow space that made me feel vulnerable. If whatever was making the noise decided to mount its attack at that moment, there wasn't much I could do. I was a sitting duck.

The closer I got to the top of the stairs the more the creaking noise sounded like footsteps. I could hear the heels of a pair of boots landing softly on the roof just outside. A shadow of a person, or what I hoped was a person, moved past the window.

I moved slowly with the crossbow ready to fire. Each step I took was deliberate and planned. I did all I could to control my breathing.

Another shadow. This time I heard a voice. Male.

My heart thumped, but that wasn't the only internal organ that reacted to the sound of the voice. The knot in my stomach was back. That meant two things. Whoever was outside on the roof was human, and... I was hungry.

"He's got one of them arrow guns," I heard someone say.

"Oz," someone else said.

I froze. I thought I recognized the voice, but it couldn't be.

"Oz, is that you?"

I felt a chill.

"Oz," the familiar voice shouted.

I hesitated and then cleared my throat before saying, "Archie?"

A door to the roof opened and in stepped a small-framed figure followed by a man of medium height and build, Bobby and Archie. I didn't move.

Archie smiled at the odd look on my face. "We ain't ghosts."

Bobby snickered. "Not hardly."

"How..." I started the question, but got lost in a muddled mess of a thousand questions I wanted to ask. I was happy as could be to see him, but at the same time, I was horrified to see him. They were human... deliciously human. *Little Bobby* I thought. *The good meat is in the little one.* I shivered and stepped back.

"Kavi, saved our butts," Archie said, looking confused by my behavior. "Took out three Délons 'fore we could blink..." He suddenly looked very sad. "She got hurt."

"Where is she?"

He pointed over his shoulder. "Out to the front of the house... dead. She led us to the ladder and made it pretty derned clear that we needed to get on the roof quick as a cat." He paused. "Something's coming."

"What?"

He shrugged. "Haven't the foggiest, but I can feel it, sure as I'm standing here."

I chuckled and then sighed. "I'm not sure you really are."

Bobby looked down at his feet and then at me. "Where do you think we're standing?"

Ignoring his Storyteller's question, Archie stepped forward. "It's us, Oz..."

I stepped back. The gnawing in my stomach was stronger than it had ever been before. "Stop."

"What..." Archie was annoyed by my request. "Gotta say I thought you'd be a little bit happier to see us."

I shook my head. "Yeah, well I would be, but... I'm kind of dealing with something myself here."

"What?" he snickered.

"The urge to eat you."

TEN

"You want to explain yourself?" Archie asked.

We had made our way down the spiral staircase. I positioned myself as far away from him and Bobby as I could. Every time they approached, I insisted that they not get any closer. I didn't just feel hunger pains when I got near him and Bobby. I actually started to salivate. I could practically taste their flesh as the longing to eat them grew stronger and stronger.

Tall Boy had not revealed himself yet. He had drifted back into a dark corner and stood as still as a statue. With his milky-white complexion, it was easy to mistake him for just that.

"It's not safe for you to be here," I said.

He chuckled. "Safe ain't something I've felt in a long, long time, Oz. Round here you got to pick and choose between what can get you killed and what can get you almost killed. Kavi seemed to think what was out there could get us killed, which means we're right where we need to be."

I rubbed my belly to try to soothe it. "I've got a feeling there isn't much of a choice this time."

He shrugged. "Appears the choice has been made. Now, you gonna get to talking or what?"

I hesitated. How do you tell someone that you've been possessed by an evil ghost? He'd believe it. There's not much you don't believe in this world. But still...

As I was about to explain the situation to Archie, I noticed a shadow move in the corridor outside the room. It startled me enough that I flinched and let out a quick yelp without even realizing it.

Archie wheeled around in the direction I was facing and drew his fists into balls. He grunted and gritted his teeth. "I hate this!"

Tall Boy moved ever so slightly and Archie saw him for the first time. He let out a savage scream and barreled toward the Throwaway.

"Stop!" I yelled, but it was too late. Archie viciously tackled Tall Boy to the ground.

Little Bobby skulked back into a dark corner.

I ran to Archie and Tall Boy. "Stop, Archie! He's with me!" I grabbed him by the back of his collar.

Archie pulled away from Tall Boy. He was breathing heavily and staring down at the strange pale Throwaway. "This is with you?"

"Yeah."

He stood, still staring at Tall Boy. "I don't understand... what got you all freaked a second ago?"

I stepped away from him as my stomach grumbled. "I... saw something." I clamped my hand on my gut and fought the hunger.

"Saw what?"

Before I could answer, the dark figure I had seen in the corridor showed itself. It was the Flish. The gray man glared and snarled.

"He with you?" Archie asked looking as uneasy as I felt.

I shook my head.

The Flish sniffed the air. "I smell a little one. Meat so tender. Meat so sweat."

"Old man," Archie said, "you come any closer and I'll plant my foot right up that bony ass of yours."

The gray man focused on Archie. "My meat! My meat! My meat to eat! That be Storyteller meat! I gnaw on Creyshaw bones after I eat the Storyteller boy!"

Archie shivered and stomped his foot. "This one of them things... the destruction things?"

"Destroyer," I corrected. "And yes."

The Flish moved toward the corner where Bobby was hiding. Archie turned and placed himself between Bobby and the gray man. I couldn't move. It was as if I was stuck in a time warp. I watched as the Flish closed in on Bobby and... hoped that he would. I wanted to watch him drag little Bobby off. I wanted to follow them. I wanted to watch the gray man strangle him and then cook him. "Sweet meat," I whispered.

Archie crouched and balled his hands into tight fists and readied himself for the fight of his life. "Little help," he said.

I nodded but still didn't move. I was afraid if I did I would help the Flish.

The old gray man stopped just out of their reach. "She kissed me on the cheek. That's when I knew I would eat her!"

Archie barked, "Back up, old man!"

"I eat the sweet Storyteller!"

Kimball started barking wildly.

"I kill the dog to eat the meat!"

No one threatens my dog. I suddenly didn't have difficulty moving. I jumped into action. "Joshua 19:9," I said rushing toward the Flish.

He turned to me. "That's my favorite."

"You told me already," I replied. I cocked my fists and was ready to fight for my dog until my last ounce of strength was gone.

The Flish backed away. "I've been gone too long. I don't have time for this. Give me the sweet Storyteller. Now!"

"Not a chance, old man," Archie said. "You want him. Come and get him."

"I do not have time!" The old gray man started to look worried. "I want the sweet meat, but I cannot stay. I cannot stay, but I want the sweet meat. I..." He smiled. "Nine days and the sweet, sweet meat is mine!" He crept backwards.

"Old man," Archie said. "If you say 'sweet meat' one more time, I'm going to..."

The Flish was gone. Vanished into the shadows.

"Where'd he...," Archie started to ask, but stopped when he noticed Tall Boy. Only Tall Boy wasn't Tall Boy any more. He was half his size, and his facial features were changing. "What's happening to him?"

I growled. "Stop! I told you not to do that."

"I am not," Tall Boy answered. His voice was much higher pitched.

"What's going on?" Archie demanded.

"What do you mean you're not doing it?" I asked.

Tall Boy raised his arm and pointed at Archie. "It is the warrior with two hearts."

The color drained from Archie's face. "Don't call me that." He turned to me. "Damn it! Tell me what's going on here."

Ignoring his plea, I asked, "Why did he call you that?"

He hesitated. "It's... Kavi called me that before... the warrior with two hearts..." He struggled to explain. "My son..."

His therapy sessions back at the facility flashed through my mind. "They took him," I said out loud, although it wasn't my intention. I was just repeating a memory... his description of what happened. "You hid in the garage... behind the hot water heater, I believe."

The blood rushed back to his face and his cheeks were almost incandescent. All he did was nod.

"You heard them screaming."

He dropped to a knee and covered his face. "I let them be take my wife and son. I did nothing."

I watched as Tall Boy continued to shrink. His face became more round. His arms chubbier. "Can't you stop this?"

Tall Boy shook his head. "It is not up to me."

"Tell me what's happening," Archie said. His eyes were red and swollen.

I cleared my throat. "Your son... He'll be with us soon."

His face froze in a look that was a cross between horrified and hopeful.

"How old was he?"

It took a long time before Archie could answer. Finally he stuttered, "Four... fo... Fourteen months."

I shook my head and glared at Tall Boy who was anything but tall by now. "You've got be kidding me. We don't have enough to deal with, and now you're going to saddle us with a fourteen-month old kid."

Archie stood. "Saddle us with... wait a minute, are you seriously saying that... that thing is turning into my son?"

I shook my head and walked as far away from them as possible. "He's your responsibility. I've got enough going on trying not to eat my friends."

"My responsibility? I've got Bobby to worry about."

"So," I said. "Now you have Bobby and... what was your son's name."

I could see the muscles in his jaw tighten. "It doesn't matter because that's not my son."

"I'll watch him," Bobby said. "I'm good with babies."

"No!" Archie shouted. "Turn him back."

I laughed. "It's not up to me."

"Turn back!" Archie screamed at Tall Boy.

Tall Boy had morphed into what looked like a five-year-old kid, and he was continuing to get smaller. His face was completely different. By the look on Archie's face, he must have taken on the general features of his son.

Archie stepped back, eyes glazed over, forehead wrinkled, and his face began to contort. I recognized that look. It was shame. He took one deep breath and whispered the name. "Max."

ELEVEN

I was hungry... no, that's not the word for it. I was fixated on eating. My every thought began with me stuffing a hunk of food in my mouth and ended with me chewing frantically, a smile on my face, grease from the fat in the meat outlining my lips. I was insane with hunger, which didn't bother me as much as what I always pictured myself eating. The meat was human... deliciously human.

I thought these thoughts as I stared at Archie. He was wiry and didn't appear to have a whole lot of meat, but I had seen the Skinner Dead eat. They always found enough meat on the bones. And all those zombie movies I had seen when the world was still normal; all those zombies loved the guts and the... brains.

Brains! The thought stuck in my head. I had forgotten about the brains. My stomach growled. I would eat the brains first... no last. Yes, last. That would be my dessert. That is how I would finish my meal.

"Stop!" I roared.

Archie looked puzzled while Little Bobby was just terrified. He held onto what was once Tall Boy but was now a baby about a year and a half old.

"Stop what?" Archie asked.

I tried to think of a believable lie to tell him because I wasn't sure how to break it to him gently that I planned on eating his brains as a sweet, scrumptious dessert. "I... can't stop... I think I was talking to myself."

"You think?"

"Forget it." I picked up my backpack and crossbow. "I have to go." Archie motioned toward me, but I halted him in his tracks by raising my hand. "Alone."

"Alone?" He grimaced. "Look, there ain't no guide book on this whole Creyshaw-warrior thing. I got no idea what I'm doing."

"None of us do."

"Yeah, but you're the only one that got your Storyteller to your Keeper."

"I was lucky." I started to exit the room.

"I need to know what to do!"

I stopped. "Stay away from me. That's what you do." I caught a glimpse of little Bobby holding the baby, and Nate's face shot up from my memory banks. "We're bad people, Archie. That's why we're here."

"What are you talking about?"

I shook my head. "You want to know how to be a good Creyshaw?"

He nodded.

"Don't matter."

He waited for me to elaborate. Finally, he threw up his hands. "That's it? Could you maybe be a little more cryptic?"

I sighed. "The way I treated Tommy, the way I made fun of him, the way I made him feel like he didn't matter... that's why he created the monsters. I mattered so much I caused the end of the world."

"But..."

"Creyshaw's don't matter, Archie. Our job is to become unnecessary. When you come up against it, when you have a decision to make, make the decision that gets you closer to not mattering."

I paused, hoping he would interject, but he was still too busy trying to process my advice.

"Lou, Wes, and the others, they want to bring back our old world. They want everything to be the way it used to be. I do, too, but..."

"But, what?" he asked.

"It scares me, too. We bring back the world and everything is how it used to be. Why would we want that? That's what got us here."

He looked at me saddened and stunned. "That is the most depressing pep talk I have ever heard."

I shrugged my shoulders. "I'm too hungry to be inspirational." I left the room with Kimball leading the way.

It took me twice as long to reach the stairs as it should have. I stopped every ten feet and fought the urge to turn around. I even made it half way back at one point. The old man had said the Storyteller's meat was sweet and tasty and... oh, how I wanted to find out. I fell into a deep trance. My mind totally focused on my hunger, and the one way I knew how to satisfy it.

"Eat the Storyteller." I said it out loud without even realizing it. Kimball barked. I heard him once, but judging by his clearly frustrated demeanor, he must have been barking for quite a while. He could sense that I wasn't myself. I was something he didn't like, but he wasn't going to give up on me. He nudged me away from the door leading back to the observation deck.

I struggled to shake the thoughts from my head and walked toward the stairs. As I walked, I got the sense that I was being followed. Archie, no doubt. He obviously didn't understand how dangerous the situation had become. I kept walking without acknowledging him. I didn't trust myself to see him and not kill him. I would be free to eat the Storyteller...

I heard the floor creak when I stopped to rub my growling

stomach. "Go back, Archie."

There was no answer.

Another creak.

"Archie!"

I stumbled forward. A large painting hung on the wall in front of me. The frame was gold and ornate. The glass protecting the painting of a Blue Ridge landscape was cracked. The crack held my attention as I followed it with my eyes from one corner to the other. That's when I saw who was following me. The pale little brunette girl dressed in black. My heart leapt up into my throat. I felt her icy cold fingers touch my arm and yelped. I rushed forward and nearly fell twice before I reached the stairs.

I sighed, relieved I had put some distance between us, but my relief was short-lived as I felt her touch again.

"What?" I shouted. I don't know why. It was as if I had heard her call my name.

She held out her hand, and I forced myself to look at her face. She wanted me to go with her. I hesitated and then slowly took her hand. The floor fell away instantly, and I slipped into a horrible darkness followed by an ultra-bright flash of light. With a thud, I hit a slab of pavement. My knees buckled and I heard a crack. The air was forced from my lungs. I wheezed and fought to catch my breath. Several seconds passed before I was able to breathe freely.

My hand on my lower back, I stretched and worked to clear the pain out of my body. That's when I first took in my new surroundings.

I was outside, but not outside the mansion. I was on a sidewalk on a busy city street. There were people everywhere. Four- and five-story buildings stretched down both sides of the block. Cars were parked along every inch of the curb. The cars were none like I had ever seen before, not in real life. I had seen them in history books. They were old... old-timey old.

People passed me on the sidewalk. It was boiling hot, but the men all wore suits and the women wore long dark dresses. The children I saw were dressed the same way. No one took any notice of me, even though I obviously didn't fit in. It was as if they didn't see me.

I walked to the corner and examined the street signs, Ninth Avenue and Fourteenth Street. A ridiculously loud car horn startled me. I turned quickly in its direction and watched the car drive down the street. I and fixated on it until I saw him. The old gray man was buying a newspaper at a newsstand. He had a small enamel pail by his feet, a box of strawberries in one hand, and something wrapped in a red and white canvas cloth tucked under his arm.

He was not the scary man from the basement. It was him, but he was different here. By the looks of it, he was having a pleasant conversation with the guy at the newsstand. I worked my way closer to the two of them so I could hear what they were saying.

"Looks like you have quite a load there, mister," the newsstand guy said.

"I can manage," the old man replied. "Although you could do me a favor."

"How so?"

The old man took the canvas-wrapped package from underneath his arm. "I'm just going up the street to a friend's house for lunch. Could I leave this package with you and then retrieve it on my way back?"

The man considered the request.

"I'll only be an hour or so," the old man said with a wink.

The man smiled and nodded. He took the package from the old man and hid it behind the newsstand. The Flish patted the man on the shoulder, picked up his pail, and turned on his heels.

I stumbled back as his eyes fell on me. My heart began to pound. I worked to find my balance and then set out in a sprint to get as far away from him as I could. Three steps into my getaway I ran into a large man dressed in a black wool suit. Actually, I ran through him. The man took no notice of me. He continued as if I wasn't there. A girl of about seven came skipping down the sidewalk begging for her daddy to wait for her. In a single hop, she too passed through me. I wasn't there. I was a ghost, but I wasn't dead. I looked at the people on the street and in the shops and in their cars from another time. They were dead. I was in the Land of the Dead.

The old man passed me, and I glanced at his newspaper. The New York Daily News, June 3, 1928.

I watched him turn the corner and resisted the urge to follow him. I didn't want to know more about him. Everything about him told me he was evil, more evil than anything I had encountered so far. I had fought a bunch of monsters and man-eating freaks, but those things were imagined into reality by tortured minds. The old gray man was different. He wasn't the invention of someone's imagination. He was real, and he lived for only one thing: his need to feed.

A little boy came around the corner in the opposite direction. He was dressed in his Sunday best. His brown hair was plastered to his skull with a thick coating of oil. It took me several seconds to recognize him as the dead boy from the pool.

He stopped a few feet in front of me, but did not acknowledge me. He just stood there.

"Can you see me?" I asked.

He turned and walked back the way he had just come.

"Why am I here?"

He stopped and turned to me, but still did not look at me. I couldn't be sure, but I think he wanted me to follow him.

"I don't want to go that way."

He looked me in the eyes. I had to follow him. I nervously tapped my hand against my leg, and then finally took the first step in his direction, followed by another and then another. Before I knew it, the boy and I had rounded the corner and we were headed up the street.

I couldn't see the old man anymore. I was relieved until I heard someone knocking on the door of a house just in front of us. The Flish stood on the front stoop, posture stiff and dignified, the paper under the arm where he had kept the package, the small crate of strawberries in his hand, the pail on the porch next to him.

The door opened and I heard a man's voice singing something about my blue heaven. I saw the silhouette of a heavyset woman standing in the doorway.

As if I were standing next to the old gray man, I heard him say, "Aw, Mr. Gene Autry and My Blue Heaven. This is the picture perfect day for such a melody, Mrs. Budd." He bent down and picked up his pail.

"Mr. Howard, so nice of you to come." She backed away and let him enter.

"Brought some of my favorite pot cheese and strawberries."

She closed the door.

It was only then I realized I was holding my breath. I let out a sigh. *If only she hadn't let him in*, I thought. *She let the monster in.*

The boy moved up the walkway to the apartment building and made his way to the front window. I milled about, not wanting to follow, but knowing I had to. I cleared my throat and joined him.

The old gray man sat in a cushioned chair across from a mild mannered man. The two men chatted while a five-year-old the woman called Beatrice read a picture book.

"How goes the farm, Mr. Howard?" The younger man asked.

"Busy, busy, busy, Mr. Budd. I'll be glad to have your boy helping me out this season."

"Well, Eddie's excited about having the work and earning some money. Good of you to make the trip out here to escort him out to the country."

"Nonsense. Glad to do it. Looking forward to Mrs. Budd's cooking."

"His name's not Howard," I said to the dead boy.

He didn't answer. He just shook his head.

I heard footsteps coming up the sidewalk and turned to see... her. The little girl from the basement. Grace. Only like the old gray man, she was different. She was happy and carefree. She hadn't seen horrible things. Hadn't lived through hell. She opened the door and entered the house.

The old man perked up when he saw her. He grinned an awful grin and stood up. "Well, who's this?"

"This, Mr. Howard," said Mr. Budd, "is our top angel, Gracie."

The old man went into a spooky trance, and stared at the girl. Grace smiled and looked away.

Mr. Budd broke the uncomfortable silence. "So, you got twenty acres do you, Mr. Howard?"

"Hmm, oh yes, twenty. Gorgeous if I do say so myself. Milking cows, Rhode Island Reds. Even got me a Swedish cook. He speaks about four words of English, but he cooks like a master chef. Got a small crew of people working for me. Don't mind telling you I've had some of them going on ten years. I try to create a family-like environment on the farm. We have picnics and potlucks. Even kin is invited. It's important to me for my workers to feel like my home is theirs."

"He came for the boy," I said.

Again, the dead boy didn't answer. He continued to shake his head.

"But he'll leave with the girl." I backed away from the window. "I don't understand why I have to see this."

The boy took my hand and tugged. In an instant, we were standing in the family's dining room. I could not tell you how we arrived there if you tortured me with a thousand needles to the eye. We were just there in a flash. The air was filled with the heavy stench of cooked cabbage. The Budd family, minus Eddie the son, and the old gray man sat at the table and clanged silverware against porcelain as they scooped up potted cheese, strawberries, ham hocks, and sauerkraut.

The old man politely ate. He had no interest in the food. Not that food anyway. He continued to stare at Grace. The family didn't seem to notice. They were so wrapped up in their food, they all jumped at the sound of the old man's voice.

"Come here, little Grace," he said, "and sit on an old man's lap." He pushed his chair away from the table.

Grace looked at her mother who in turned looked at the man she knew as Mr. Howard. He smiled warmly. She nodded to her daughter to do as the man asked.

Grace stood and slowly approached the old gray man. He reached down, picked her up, and placed her on his lap. He looked like he was about to drool all over himself. For the first time, I wished I could do more than just watch. I so wanted to belong to that time so I could deck the old man. Beat him within an inch of his life. I couldn't believe her parents just sat there and took it in. Didn't they see that their daughter was in the hands of an evil monster?

The old man reached in his pocket pulled out a stack of cash. "Sweetie, do Uncle Howard a favor and count out the money for me." He laid out the money on the table. "Hold on. Got some pocket change, too." He let the coins fall on the wood surface of the table.

Grace's eyes opened wide at the sight of so much money. Her parents stopped eating mid-chew, and watched with anticipation as Grace counted out the bills. Mrs. Budd even managed a smile, although I'm not sure she was aware of it. No one in the Budd family had ever seen so much money.

"Ninety-two dollars and fifty cents," Grace proclaimed.

"Well by golly, that is fifty cents too much."

"It is?" Grace asked.

"Got plenty I can do with $92, but I can't think of one thing I can do with that extra fifty cents."

Grace considered the matter. "You could buy some candy."

He chuckled. "I suppose I could, but these old teeth of mine can't handle candy. If I only knew someone with young enough teeth that liked candy."

"I like candy," Beatrice barked.

"And her teeth are the youngest here," Grace added.

"Now that's an idea." He winked at Mrs. Budd. "I tell you what, Grace. Why don't you take those coins and buy some candy for you and your sister down at the corner store."

Beatrice sat up straight like she had been shocked to life. Grace looked at her father for permission.

"Do as Mr. Howard says," Mr. Budd said. "Take Beatrice with you. Mind the streets and stick to the walk."

Grace jumped off the old man's lap, but he grabbed her skinny arm before she could get too far away. "Give Uncle Howard a little kiss on the cheek."

Grace recoiled and then relented. She quickly leaned in and gave him a peck on the cheek.

The old man's eyes lit up.

Grace pulled away, took her sister's hand, and bolted for the front door.

The children gone, the adults settled into a series of friendly conversations about farming, about Mr. Budd's job as a doorman, about church and God and a trip to China Mr. Howard had taken years ago.

"Awful country, that," he said sipping some coffee.

"Really? I always find the Orientals so pleasant," Mrs. Budd said, spreading some sweet cheese on a hard roll.

"The ones in this country, I agree," the old man said. "But over there, the economy is in such a state, the poor people are forced to live like animals."

"How so?" Mr. Budd asked.

The old man cocked his head to the right. "I'm afraid most of what they do I can't repeat at the supper table, especially one as fine as this with such lovely occupants." He gave a nod to Mrs. Budd causing her to blush.

"Come on now, Mr. Howard," Mr. Budd pleaded. "The Mrs. and I haven't had much opportunity to travel abroad and most likely won't ever get to. Share one fact with us."

The old man began to speak, but stopped abruptly. He turned to Mrs. Budd. "Only with the lady's permission."

She seemed taken aback by his refinement. I wanted to puke because I knew it was an act. She blushed again and nodded.

"Very well." The old man leaned back. "Wages are small and meat is scarce. People are literally starving to death. It's an ugly way to die, Mrs. Budd. I wouldn't wish it on anybody. I suppose we can't judge them too harshly for what they've been reduced to doing." He gulped his coffee and didn't continue.

"What would that be, Mr. Howard?" Mr. Budd asked

The old man had gone into a trance state again. He shook iit off. "Hmmm, oh no, Mr. Budd. It's too horrid."

Mrs. Budd looked as if she were preparing herself to be

repulsed. Her brow was furrowed and eyes had narrowed. Her head was turned slightly to the right as if she was trying to minimize the impact of the ending to the old man's story. "You may continue, Mr. Howard. I'll be all right."

He reached out and patted her hand. "Just remember, I'm telling this story against my better judgment."

"We will hold you blameless, Mr. Howard," Mr. Budd said. "Rest assured."

The old gray man cleared his throat. He surveyed the room and fixed his gaze on me. My mouth went dry. Surely he couldn't see me. I was standing behind Mr. Budd, so maybe it just seemed like he was looking at me. I saw a small smile form on his face and then it quickly disappeared.

"They sell children under twelve as meat."

The sentence cut through the air and shattered the innocent feel of the Budd house. Nothing so evil had ever been spoken in the home before. Mrs. Budd covered her mouth with her hand.

Mr. Budd fidgeted in his chair. "That can't be true," he said.

"I'm afraid it is. A business associate saw it with his own eyes."

"Saw?" Mrs. Budd reflexively asked.

"Walked into a butcher shop to order veal."

"So," Mr. Budd said.

"The door to the back room opened and he saw... a boy, cut in half hanging from a meat hook like beef cattle."

Mrs. Budd screamed.

The old man reached out and gently grabbed her hand. "I warned you it was ugly. I'll have you know I went to the authorities there and reported the incident. I was as outraged as you are now."

"What happened?" Mr. Budd asked.

"I was escorted to the nearest port and put on a ship to New

Zealand."

"I don't understand," Mrs. Budd said.

"The Chinese government knows about the deplorable practice, Mrs. Budd. They allow it to go on. I've written the governor of New York, my congressman, even sent a telegram to the president. I've never gotten a response. I suppose they think it's too sensational to be true." He sipped his coffee.

"What about your business associate?" Mr. Budd asked. "If he were to back up your claims..."

"That isn't possible, Mr. Budd."

"Why?"

The old man sighed as if he were in great emotional pain. "He was in the country for six months. When you're in a foreign country that long, you develop a lot of the local customs and way of living."

"What are you saying?" Mrs. Budd asked.

He frowned. "I think you know, madam."

"No," Mr. Budd said.

"Yes," the old man replied.

"He ate the meat?" Mr. Budd asked just so there was no misunderstanding.

"Worse than that. He developed a taste for it. I got a horrible letter from him describing how wonderfully sweet the meat is. I shredded the letter to pieces it so incensed me. I tell you, if I ever lay eyes on him... Children are precious, Mrs. Budd. I treasure them. You can't blame me for what I would do to that man." Tears started to flow down his cheek.

I stood in awe of the old man's performance. He even convinced me he was disgusted by the thought of eating children, and I knew what he really was. The Budds didn't have a chance.

Mrs. Budd reached across the table and patted his hand. "Mr. Howard, don't dare tell me the man's name because I would hunt him down in a week's time and make him pay in the most painful way possible."

The old man looked at Mrs. Budd with surprise and then started with a small chuckle that turned into a hardy laugh. The Budds joined in. They were so enjoying themselves that they didn't notice when Grace and Beatrice returned with their brother Eddie and his friend Willie Korman.

The children stood at the edge of the room and watched in amazement as the adults yucked it up. Mrs. Budd was the first to acknowledge them.

"You're late," she said to Eddie.

"We got a game of stickball going. Went long."

"Mr. Howard's a busy man, boys," Mr. Budd said. "Can't make him wait like that."

"Sorry, Mr. Howard," the boys said in unison.

He waved them off. "Nonsense. Who's your friend, Eddie?"

"This is Willie Korman, sir. He's strong. Seen him lift fifty pounds over his head."

"Is that so?"

"Yes, sir," Willie said.

"We was wondering if you could use him on the farm, too, Mr. Howard."

"You were, were you?" The old man examined the boy. "I'll have to have a talk with his parents."

"They don't mind," Willie said.

"I'm sure they don't, but I can't have them reporting me for kidnapping," the old man laughed. He pulled out his pocket watch. "I've got time to visit your house before I go back to the country. In fact, I just found out yesterday my sister is having a birthday party for my niece this afternoon, and I won't be heading back until tomorrow."

"Tomorrow?" Eddie said sounding disappointed.

The old man laughed. "The boy is certainly anxious to start earning money."

"He looks at it as an adventure," Mrs. Budd said.

"Indeed." The old man pulled the money out of his pocket again and handed two dollars to Eddie. "Round up all your friends and see a picture show on me. You and I will head over to Willie's house in the morning and then we'll start your adventure."

Eddie stared at the money as if it were a pot of gold. "Whoa." He unintentionally yanked the money out of the old man's gnarled hands. The two boys exited the house giggling the whole way.

The old man stood. "I should be going. My sister is expecting me." He took one last sip of his coffee, smiled and then did a half turn toward the door to the hallway before he stopped. "Say, I just had a thought." He reached in his pocket and pulled out a slip of paper. "My niece is Grace's age. This party is going to be full of little girls just like her. I would be the hit of the party if I brought more than my brittle old bones."

The Budds were thrown by the request. They looked at each other for guidance. Each one wanting to defer to the other.

Mrs. Budd said, "I don't know. Grace doesn't usually like to take trips."

"I'll be her escort," the old man said. "No need to worry. She'll have the time of her life. There will be cake and ice cream, and a pony..."

"A pony?" Grace said excitedly.

"That's too much trouble for you, Mr. Howard," Mr. Budd argued.

"I'd enjoy the company on the train." He looked at the paper. "My sister lives in a nice building on Columbus Avenue, 137th street."

There was a moment of silence while the Budds considered it.

I darted from Mrs. Budd to Mr. Budd screaming at the top my lungs. "Don't let her go! Don't do it! Please, don't let her go!" Of course, they couldn't hear me, but I thought if I could just shout loud enough, some part of the message would break through.

Mrs. Budd smiled. "C'mon, Grace. Let's get you in your party dress."

I rushed to the dead boy and yanked him up by his collar. "Why am I here? Let me help her!"

He did what he did best, gave me a cold, pointless stare.

"I don't understand what I am supposed to do." I released him and was only mildly surprised to find that my location had changed. I was no longer in the Budds' home. I was standing next to the newsstand. The operator was holding the old man's package. He wanted to open it. I could see it in his eyes. I wanted him to open it.

A girl giggled and startled the newsstand operator. He quickly put the package back from where he had retrieved it. The giggle belonged to Grace. The old gray man was guiding her down the street. He had not seen the operator examining his package. He was too enthralled by the little girl.

"Enjoy your lunch, sir?"

"Indeed I did."

"I see you picked up a pretty young friend."

"The prettiest. We're on our way to a party."

"My, doesn't that sound grand. A fine day for it."

"Yes," the old gray man said. He was growing impatient. He wanted to be on his way. He wanted to get to... it. "You still have my package, I trust."

"I do." The newsstand operator bent down and picked up the package. "Is this for the party?"

"No," the old man said.

"The girl, then?"

The old man shook his head.

"It's a secret, is it?"

The old gray man stiffened. He scowled and shot darts with his eyes at the newsstand worker. "These are my tools of the trade. I'd be lost without them." He shoved the package under his arm and took Grace's hand.

The newsstand operator felt the same fear I'd felt in the basement of the Biltmore. I could see it in his face. He knew just as I did that Grace was being led to her death, and he knew that death would be more horrific than anyone could ever imagine. He felt it in his bones.

I stood inches from the newsstand operator's face and shouted, "Stop them!" If I could just shout loud enough, he could hear me. I knew it. "You know what's going to happen to her! Stop them! Please!"

He followed the old gray man and Grace in a desperate stare until they disappeared around the corner. He sighed, pulled his stool closer, and sat down. He ran a shaky hand through his sweat-drenched hair and then examined both hands. In a low whisper he said, "The devil's tools."

DAY 2

TWELVE

I woke up to a voice whispering "devil's tools" in my ear. I lay at the bottom of the stairs leading up to the fourth floor. I didn't remember descending them. I slowly became aware of a series of dull pains shooting through my back to my knees and then to my head. I was hurting and if I had to guess why, I'd say I fell down the stairs.

I sat up gingerly. I tested the areas that hurt the most for broken bones. As far as I could tell, everything was intact. Rubbing the back of my head, I found a good sized lump that was tender to the touch, but it was nothing I couldn't deal with on my own.

What had happened to me? I had been at the top of the stairs... the girl in black grabbed my hand... the ground fell away. Had I just fallen down the stairs? Knocked myself out and had some weird hallucination while I was unconscious? Is that all it was?

No, I was there. I had gone to the Land of the Dead. I was sure of it. I had seen the Flish, the Budds... Grace. I don't know what I was supposed to do with the information, but I had no doubt that I was actually there.

I heard a crackle, pop, and then a hiss. I recognized it immediately. Someone was calling me on my two-way. The problem was .. where was my two-way? I scanned my surroundings and had difficulty focusing in the dark. I crawled around the immediate area on my hands and knees and listened carefully. "Oz?" a voice said through a wave of static. I placed my hand in front of me and felt the nylon fabric of the backpack. Frantically and clumsily, I opened the pack and pulled out the two-way.

"Go for Oz," I sighed.

"I think... Ty... April." I didn't recognize the voice. The static was heavy. I couldn't make out every word.

"Say again."

"Tyrone... insane... April... eat her." I heard a scream through the crackling.

"Who is this? Where are you?"

The voice came again. It was Lou. She talked slowly and deliberately this time. "I heard... Tyrone... on the radio. It sounds like... he has April. He's going to... eat her... winter garden."

"Winter garden?" I couldn't think straight. What winter garden? Then it hit me. The main floor, it was a glassed indoor garden. "I'll go. Just stay clear."

I heard another scream through the radio followed by a roar from Ajax. "Stop..." was the last thing I heard.

I stood, shook off the stiffness from the pain, and prepared to make my way down to Lou as quickly as possible. A small figure darted out of a nearby corner and wobbled toward me. It was a boy, a small smiling boy. A large, white furry mass followed closely behind him. Tarek. That meant the boy must have been...Nate. My Storyteller. He was walking. He could barely keep his head up by himself when I'd last seen him. He had grown so much and so fast. I was elated. Not because I hadn't seen him in such a long time. I was elated because I was hungry, and this small boy would hit the spot. I took a step toward him and was quickly knocked on my backside by Tarek, the Keeper who had helped me defeat the Takers.

"Back, boy," he groaned. His voice rumbled like a high powered race car. "You stink of the Flish."

My gut twisted and I doubled over from a jolt of hunger pains. "Why are you here? Why did you bring him here?"

"He goes where I go," Tarek said. "I came here to tell you it's not safe for you here."

"You think?" I said sarcastically. "Thanks for the tip."

He ignored my tone. "You think this is something you can beat. You can't. The Flish isn't like the other Destroyers."

I tried to inch my way toward Nate without Tarek noticing. I thought if I moved ever so slightly every few seconds the big beast wouldn't see until I was close enough to pounce and get one small bite of the sweet, sweet Storyteller meat. "What makes him different?"

"The other Destroyers, they are impossible yet they exist. They shouldn't be, but they are. That is their weakness. They are cruel because they were imagined that way. That is their limitation. The Flish is cruel because he was born that way. He was meant to be. He once served a purpose, a horrific and terrifying purpose, but a purpose nonetheless. He has no limitations." Tarek scooped the youngster up in his enormous hands and shielded him from me. "You have to leave, Oz Griffin."

"I can't," I said feeling greatly disappointed that Nate was impossible to get to.

"Why?"

I thought about the question. The truth was, I wasn't sure why I couldn't leave. I had thought it was because I had to find the Land of the Dead, but I was pretty sure I had just been there. The smart thing to do would be to call the others on the two-way and leave... I looked at the radio. "Lou. She's in trouble."

Tarek grumbled. "Why was I stuck with such a stubborn and stupid warrior? She will be in greater trouble if you get close enough to smell her. You're infected by the Flish."

"I won't hurt her. I can't hurt her. She's my..." I didn't know how to finish that sentence so I left it undone.

"She's nothing but a meal to you now."

"Shut up!" I barked. "Don't say that!"

"The Flish gets in. That's what he does."

I bent over, placed my hands on my knees, and breathed deeply. It was getting harder and harder to hold back from making an attempt to get at Nate. I could hear him giggling. It was driving me mad. "Help me beat him."

"I cannot."

"Don't give me that 'this is not my fight' crap..."

"That's not it," he interrupted. "I don't know how to beat him. He is the end, Oz Griffin."

"What about the warrior... Creyshaw for this story?"

"Dead. Consumed by the Flish..."

"Consumed?" I said. "His Storyteller then..."

"Held by the Délons, but not for long. The Flish will find him and consume him as well. When he does, every human, every Destroyer, every warrior, every Storyteller... even the Keepers will be infected by the Flish."

"How? He's stuck in this house as far as I can tell."

"For now, but he will chip away at your resolve day after day until the weakest of you will succumb to the urges of the infection and eat the others. Then the Flish will no longer be bound to this house."

I rubbed my rumbling stomach. "So what do you want me to do?"

"Leave. Now."

"If we leave now the infection will go away?"

He paused. "No."

"No? So, I'll always feel this..." I got another glimpse of Nate.

"Hunger?"

Tarek couldn't bring himself to look me in my eyes. "You will."

"And the others?"

"None of you can purge yourself of the need to feed. The only way is to survive the nine days, and there is no way to survive the nine days. Not even you, Oz Griffin.

"But," he said, "you can't spread the infection if you leave now. It is only spread by the Flish through his surviving host."

I was confused. "How do you expect us to work together out there if we're always trying to eat each other?"

He looked away without answering.

"Wait a minute," I said. "Are you saying we have to split up? Forever?"

"That is not what I'm saying."

I felt momentarily relieved.

"The others cannot be allowed to leave," he said.

I processed his statement in my head. "But you just said the longer they stay..." I practically swallowed my tongue when I realized what he wanted me to do. "No. I won't. I can't. They are my family."

"You don't have a choice. They cannot be allowed to leave."

"But I can?"

"Apparently your work is not yet done. You have more to do."

"Forget it," I said angrily "It's not an option. There has to be another way."

He looked away again, and I thought I detected something in his face.

"What?"

He didn't answer.

"If you know something... anything... another way..."

"I don't know enough," he yelled.

"What does that mean?"

"It means I know only enough to give you hope and hope is your enemy. Hope will make you do foolish things. Hope will be your undoing."

"Tell me what you know!"

He growled, and it rattled my bones.

I shook it off and said, "You're wrong, Tarek. It's not my undoing. It's what keeps me going. I am nothing without it, so you might as well tell me what you know."

He mumbled something about useless humans and then said, "If you can bind him to this story's Keeper, he will be powerless, and it is said that the infection will disappear. That's all I know."

"Who's the Keeper?"

"As I said, that is all I know."

I nodded. "How do I bind him to his keeper?"

He groaned. "As I said..."

I stopped. "That is all you know. It's something. I can use it."

Tarek slipped back into the darkness. "You will use it to your detriment," he said. "Good-bye, Oz Griffin."

THIRTEEN

Staring Tyrone in the face, I suddenly didn't object to killing him and the others as much as I did before. Cutting him up, and making a stew out of him actually seemed like the best idea I had ever had.

Tyrone was thinking the same thing about me. That's how this infection worked. People eat delicious people. It doesn't matter if you're friends, or fighting a war together, or if it's some kid you saved from a Taker, and he did the same for you. You just wanted to eat him... needed to eat him.

Lou was safe. Or at least I thought she was. I didn't see her, but Ajax had positioned himself between Tyrone and the back area of the Winter Gardens. He was clearly protecting something. I suspected he was protecting Lou from Tyrone and the other way around, too.

"Come to save your girlfriend, Oz?" Tyrone's voice was hurried and desperate.

"Came to save you," I said. "And she's not my girlfriend."

"Whatever," he answered. "She's breakfast as far I'm concerned. I'll have April for lunch, and if you don't get out of here, I'll have you for dinner."

I looked up at the towering glass dome ceiling. The dim morning light hovered overhead. I had not realized a whole night had passed. That meant we had eight more days.

I heard a whimpering over my left shoulder and slowly turned toward it. Through the dying branches of a potted tree, I saw a set of eyes looking back at me. Blonde hair fell across a sweat drenched forehead. I stepped closer to get a better look. It was...
"Valerie?"

Tyrone groaned. "A cheap knock off."

A Throwaway version of her, of course. I strained to get a good look at her through the dead branches. It had been so long since I had seen Valerie. This version of her was so much taller than what I remembered. She was made as Tyrone imagined her. I felt a sadness for him that I hadn't allowed myself to feel until now. He loved her. They seemed too young to even know what love was, but looking at the Throwaway version of Valerie, it was obvious that she was pieced together by blissfully happy memories. In the middle of the destruction that was our lives, Tyrone found and fell in love with the girl of his dreams. It seemed absurdly impossible.

I heard the shuffling of feet following the rapid patter of shoes on the hard floor. Something or someone struck me from behind and shoved me to the floor before I could react. Whoever or whatever it was snarled like an animal. I felt the feathery touch of hair float across the back of my neck.

I jerked hard enough to knock the attacker off my back, and wasn't totally surprised to see that it was April who crashed to the floor. I jumped up and prepared for another attack. It didn't come. She snapped and growled like she was possessed, and she was. We all were.

"This is crazy," I said desperately trying to control my breathing. "We can't do this to each other."

Lou's voice came out of the darkness. "And I will cause them to eat the flesh of their sons and the flesh of their daughters, and they shall eat every one the flesh of his friend in the siege and straitness, wherewith their enemies, and they that seek their lives, shall straiten them."

Throwaway Valerie stepped out of her hiding place. "I want to leave this house."

"We can't," I said.

"Why?" Tyrone asked. To his credit, he was showing as much restraint as I was. He wanted to attack me, but he was using every bit of his willpower to stay put.

"I wish I could answer that," I said. "But we were brought here for a reason. I can't leave until I figure out what that reason is."

"You can't," April said sounding as if she might hyperventilate. "But we can."

"We need each other," Lou said.

"She's right," I said

"We're going to kill each other," April barked.

I shook my head. "Beyond this place." I pointed toward the front door. "Out there. We fight together. We can't let this place drive us apart."

"That would sound a lot better if I could stop picturing myself stringing you up by your feet and gutting you like a deer," Tyrone said. "No offense."

"None taken," I said. "I feel the same way..." I stopped mid-sentence when I saw myself approaching from the back of the gardens. "What the...?"

Lou stepped out from behind... me or a version of me. "We have to make a pact."

"What's going on?" I asked.

Tyrone giggled. "Looks like your girlfriend replaced you."

I looked closer. He was right. Lou's Throwaway had become me, a slightly distorted version of me, but it was still a passable rendition of me.

"I didn't do it," Lou insisted. "It just happened."

"That's the way it works," Tyrone said. "They become what you want. Pretty clear what you want."

Lou gave him a vicious glare. "What I want is for you to shut the hell up..."

"You said something about a pact," I said trying to avoid an attack by... anyone in the room on anyone else in the room.

She hesitated and then addressed the bigger issue at hand. "The dead brought us here for a reason. I agree with you. There's something here that will help us get home."

"So," April said.

"So we can't leave until we find it."

"But your boyfriend says we got nine days," Tyrone said.

"I didn't say it," I corrected. "Grace did. The girl. The ghost... and stop calling me her boyfriend."

Lou looked hurt by my last statement. She shook it off and carried on. "Then we have nine days..."

"Eight now," I said.

"Eight days," she said. "We have to agree not to..." She should have ended the sentence with 'eat each other,' but she didn't. She searched desperately for an ending that wasn't so gruesome. "... stay out of each other's way."

I chuckled absentmindedly. "That's easier said than done."

"Yeah," April piped in. "It's taking everything I have to not jump on Oz right now and rip open his throat." She licked her lips.

"Do you want to go home?" Lou asked.

We all waited for the others to reply. Finally, we just tentatively nodded our heads in unison.

"Then we have got to make this pact. We get away from each other... far away, and we look for whatever it is the dead brought us here to find."

"If we don't know what is we're looking for, how will we know when we find it?" April asked.

"You'll know," I said. "Pretty sure of that."

"If one of us breaks the pact?" Tyrone asked.

"One of us won't," Lou said. "We can't."

"But if we do?" he asked.

"Stop asking..." Lou started but I cut her off.

"He's right. There have to be consequences for breaking the pact."

"Not making it back home isn't good enough?" she asked.

We didn't answer.

She threw up her hands. "Fine." She turned to Ajax whose hackles were up, but otherwise managed to keep a fairly cool demeanor. She went through a series of signs, and he shook his hea side to side. She signed again. He shook his head more emphatically. A grunt came from behind April, and Ariabod knuckle-walked forward with Throwaway June tagging closely behind. Ariabod signed to Lou. She signed back and then let out a sigh of relief. Clearly he agreed to do what Ajax had refused to do.

"What?" Tyrone asked.

"He's your consequence," Lou said.

"Meaning?" April asked.

"Meaning Ariabod has agreed to kill the first one of us to break the pact." The look of relief vanished from her face as the words left her mouth. It was as if it had just dawned on her what the gorilla had agreed to do.

"The first one of us? What happens after that?"

She slowly shook her head. "Does it matter?"

Tyrone shrugged. "I guess not."

"What about Wes and Gordy?" I asked. "They have to agree to the pact, too."

She nodded and held up her two-way. "I'll take care of Wes. You can convince Gordy."

"We're assuming the fat man hasn't already eaten Gordy," April said.

We all looked at her not because what she said was outrageous, but because it was a possibility none of us had thought of.

"There's something else," I added. "Archie and Bobby, they're here."

"What?" April said excitedly.

I had been so racked by hunger and guilt for wanting to eat my friends that I had almost forgotten no one else knew they were here. The others almost looked genuinely relieved to learn that they were safe, at least from the Délons and the other Destroyers outside the house.

"They showed up last night," I said. "They're all right."

"I want to see them," April said.

"Not a good idea. You should wait until we make it out of this place."

She snickered. "I doubt I'll make it out of this place."

"You shouldn't say that," I said.

"Don't tell me what to do."

"If you don't think you're going to make it out of here," I said, "that means you have no incentive to keep the pact. If you're not planning on keeping the pact, I'm going to suggest we let Ariabod kill you now to save us from going through a lot of drama."

"What... no, I didn't mean..." She stomped her foot. "I'm tired, and I'm hungry, and you all smell... you know... edible. I just want to see Archie and Bobby. They're kind of like my family"

I felt bad for being so harsh with her. "I get that, but trust me, you don't want to see them like this. If you think we smell edible, wait until you get a whiff of a Storyteller."

She licked their lips.

"So what's the plan?" Tyrone asked.

"We split up again," I said "We check in with one another every hour on our radios. That way we'll know we're all alive and we'll be able to keep tabs on everyone's locations so we don't run into each other."

"Remember," Lou said, "we were brought here for a reason. Keep an eye out for anything that might help us figure out what that reason is. The quicker we know, the quicker we can get out of here and back home."

We all agreed and stood in uncomfortable silence before finding the strength and courage to walk away.

***

I stopped in the master bedroom on the second floor before going back up to the fourth floor. I felt like my best bet was to write a brief note explaining the pact to Archie. That way, I wouldn't have to get involved in any long conversations that would test my need to feed.

I rifled through the drawers of the dresser and didn't find anything to write with or on. I looked in every nook and cranny and directed Kimball to sniff around. I was fairly certain he didn't understand me, but you never knew in this backwards universe. Maybe Kimball did understand English. I wouldn't have been surprised if he just started talking one day.

I found a closet in the back of the room. I hesitated before opening it. There was a very real possibility that I would be extremely sorry that I opened the door to the closet. As I said, you just didn't know what you were going to find in this universe. I held my breath, opened the door, and quickly stepped back in a crouching position. Nothing. I breathed out and slowly poked my head past the doorway. It was a big closet. Not as big as some of those fancy walk-in closets I used to see on TV, but it was big enough for a safe and three filing cabinets.

I whistled for Kimball, and he came running over. "Stay here. Watch the door."

He tilted his head and then panted, revealing a soothing canine smile. I patted him on the head and stepped into the closet. I opened the top drawer of the first filing cabinet and found nothing but files, mostly maintenance records. I opened the second drawer and found files filled with photos. I started looking through them. I'm not exactly sure why, but I felt the need. If I had been paying attention, I would have noticed the light slowly getting dimmer in the closet, but for some reason I was fixated on the pictures. Most of the pictures were just photos of the grounds at the mansion.

I turned to the door. "Kimball..." I heard a bark just before the door slammed shut.

I felt the breath of a disembodied child on my earlobe as it said, "The boogeyman got him."

A brilliant flash of light momentarily blinded me. It took several seconds for my eyes to adjust and refocus. As things cleared, it became apparent to me that I was no longer in the closet. I was in a poorly lit hallway.

The short red and brown carpet was marked by the impressions of little footprints. I heard the sound of children laughing close by. I followed the prints down the hallway with my eyes until they rounded the corner. I had no interest in following them because I was back in the Land of the Dead, and that could mean only one thing. I was here to witness something I had no power to stop.

The dead boy stepped out of a darkened doorway just beyond the entrance of the adjoining hallway. He looked at me and then turned his attention in the direction of the laughter. My own voice sounded off in my head, *Eight Days.*

I slowly began to walk towards him. Just as I was about to reach the corner, I heard rushed footsteps behind me. Before I could turn to investigate, a boy of about twelve passed through me. I gasped. My stomach dropped as if I was on a rollercoaster plunging down the first big hill on the track.

"What'cha kiddies up to you?" the boy asked.

I rounded the corner and saw that he was talking to two much younger boys, only three or four years of old. They shrugged and seemed a little frightened of the older boy.

"Cat got your tongues, eh?"

Again they just shrugged.

"My baby sister's asleep, so I got some time to play while she's out. What'cha wanna do?"

"We was playing rock, paper, scissors," the skinnier of the two boys said.

"That's kid's stuff," the older boy said.

"We're kids," the chubbier boy said.

The older boy hesitated and then smiled. "We should look for the ghost."

The two younger boys stiffened and stared at each other with terror in their eyes.

"What ghost, Johnny?" the skinnier boy said.

The older boy sat down on the floor and leaned against the wall. "You ain't heard about the ghost in this hallway?"

The two younger boys shook their heads.

"Goodness, I just figured your folks would tell you about it to keep you from gettin' et up."

"Et up?" the chubbier boy asked.

"Yeah, some people 'round here think it could even be the boogeyman. How old are you Billy B?"

The chubby boy held up three fingers.

"What about you Billy G?"

"Four," the skinny boy answered.

"That explains why you ain't never heard about it." He patted the floor and invited the boys to sit down, which they did. "About five years ago..." He looked up and down the hallway. "I think it was on this very floor. There was this boy... I think he was three or four just like you guys. Anyway, he was playing and having a grand old time on a day a lot like this when these lights started to flicker on and off." He pointed to the half dozen lights lining both walls." He didn't think nothing of it at first, and then he heard footsteps . . . thud, thud, thud . . . coming down the hall, 'cept there weren't nobody there." The two Billys sat with their mouths open, soaking up every word. "He kept on about his playing and then another thud came. And another. Well, this little boy wasn't scared of nothin'."

"He wasn't?" Billy B said.

"Not hardly anyway." The bigger boy shifted and leaned forward. "He decided he would go looking for whoever was coming down the hall. He got about five steps into his search when the lights went completely off. Boom! It was completely dark." The two Billys jumped.

A baby cried in the distance and the older boy sat up. "Shoot. That's my baby sister." He stood up.

"Where you going?" Billy G asked.

"My ma ain't home. I'm supposed to be watching after my baby sister. She went down for her nap. I thought she'd be out until ma got home."

"What about the boogeyman?" Billy B asked.

"Did he et the boy?" Billy G asked.

The older boy smiled. "Cooked him up like a roast. Put his guts in a pie and sold it at the church bizarre. Who do you think bought that pie?"

The two smaller boys shrugged.

"The boy's daddy. Said it was the best pie he ever et. Jumped out the window when the police told him he et his own son in a pie." The sound of the baby crying interrupted his story again, and he started to jog down the hall. He stopped to give them one last detail. "Police found a note on the window sill wrote by the man. It said he was jumping because all he could think about was having another slice of that pie." The older boy darted down the hallway and burst through the door to the stairwell. I saw him take his first two steps up before the door closed. I turned to the dead boy. "Tell me what I'm supposed to do. I'm running out of time. My friends are in danger. Just tell me."

The dead boy turned in my direction but looked past me. I followed his gaze and was horrified to see the gray man step out of the shadows at the other end of the hall. He was coming straight towards me, his eyes fixed on me. The terrible thought went through my head that he could see me. His heavily wrinkled brow hung low as he approached. His gait was quick and deliberate. I spotted the package under his arm. In a matter of seconds he reached me and didn't slow as he passed right through me. I felt an ice cold chill zip through my body. He turned down the adjoining hallway and didn't break his stride as he approached the two Billys.

The two small boys saw him and seemed startled. They gasped and stepped back as the old man approached. I couldn't see his face, but I could feel him smile. His face changed. The gray man hid underneath a kindly grandfather mask.

"Hello, boys," he said.

The boys didn't reply.

"I'm Mr. Howard. Got a sister that lives in this building. She's got a little girl about your age in fact."

The boys looked as if they were starting to relax.

"You wouldn't know her, would you?"

The boys looked at each and then Billy G said, "No."

"They're having a party up on the roof," the Flish said.

My heart sank, and I started to shake. I don't know why. I knew where I was. This wasn't happening. This was the Land of the Dead. This was just some sick and twisted recording of how people died. I was going to watch these two boys die. The thought of it brought tears to my eyes. I tried to tell myself that it wasn't real, but it didn't matter.

"They're having cake and ice cream, and all the boys are going to get baseballs just for coming," the old man said laying it on thick.

The two boys' faces lit up. I could just see the thoughts soaring through their little heads. *Ice cream! Baseballs!*

The old man scratched his head. "Trouble is I can't find how to get up to the roof. I'd hate to miss the party."

"There's a ladder that goes up," Billy G said. "My daddy showed me once."

"Really?" the Flish asked excitedly.

Billy B pointed to the package under the old man's arm. "That a present for the party?"

The old man chuckled. "No. These are my tools."

"The devil's tools," I said.

"You boys wouldn't want to show me where this ladder is, would you? I'm pretty sure I can get you into the party."

The boys didn't answer.

"There's a baseball in it for each of you."

Billy B looked amazed. "Really?"

The old man nodded. "Yep, and cake and ice cream, too."

That was all it took. Billy B grabbed Billy G's hand and they led the old man down the hallway. They passed two feet from me. I wanted to scoop them up and run far away, but I couldn't. I just had to watch. The Flish passed by me, and I nearly passed out when he winked at me. He knew I was there. He knew I was watching. He liked it.

The dead boy followed them, but I refused to do the same. He turned to me and waited. I shook my head. He opened his mouth and spoke in my voice, repeating the words I had spoken earlier, "I'm running out of time. My friends are in danger."

I followed the dead boy through the door and up the stairs. The old man and the two Billys were a floor ahead of us. Johnny opened the door from his floor as we passed. He didn't even hesitate. He bounded down the steps to the floor below and went back to rejoin his two little friends, but they would be nowhere to be found.

The dead boy picked up the pace, and I struggled to keep up. He wasn't just moving faster. He was frantic. It was as if he didn't want to miss a thing, or maybe he didn't want me to miss a thing.

We reached the top floor just in time to see the old man climbing a ladder to the roof with some difficulty. His tools were getting in the way. He stopped every rung to adjust and reposition the package under his arm. Just as he reached the top rung, he dropped the package and it hit the floor with a metallic clank. The fabric cover twisted on one of the rungs on the way down and was pulled free from the metal box. The lid popped open as it bounced on the tile floor, and his tools scattered. This is what I was supposed to see. The old man climbed down the ladder like he was a world class athlete. It was as if we were in the basement of the Biltmore again. He moved with purpose. He knelt down and picked up a small knife. His eyes shifted from the knife to me. He gave me a dreadful smile.

"Trimming knife," he said carefully placing the knife in the metal box.

I backed away. Was he talking to me? Could he see me?

He picked up a bigger knife and placed it in the box. "Utility knife."

"What..." I started but stopped when he interrupted me with a blood chilling snicker.

"My favorite," he said picking up a knife that looked like a small machete. "Cimeter knife. Great for cutting up meat. Young meat is tender. Gives way to this blade with beautiful ease. It's poetry."

Billy G peaked over the portal leading to the roof. "Mister, where's the party?"

"Be right up, boys." He hurriedly gathered up the rest of the tools: a small bone saw, a sharpening steel, another knife, and a pair of scissors.

"Why are you doing this?" I asked.

He acted as if he didn't hear me. Every tool back in the metal box, he closed it and wrapped it in its fabric cover. He climbed up the ladder, and just before he stepped through the portal to the roof, he looked down and said, "I'm hungry."

I looked at the dead boy. He cast his eyes down. "Why aren't we following?"

He didn't answer of course.

I wanted to slap him, but knew it wouldn't do any good. He was ashamed. He slowly started to walk down the stairs.

"No," I barked. "We can't just let him do this. Help me stop him!"

The boy didn't acknowledge my plea. He continued down the stairs.

I growled. I wasn't going to let this happen. I zipped up the ladder quicker than I had ever climbed anything in my life. Standing on the rough sheets of roofing, absorbing the brisk breeze, I spotted the Flish and the two boys near the edge of the building. I hurried towards them. The old man was in perfect position. I could rush him and send him tumbling off the roof. I had lost count of the floors as we followed them up the stairs, but I guessed we were six or seven stories up.

He must have read my mind because he looked at me and said, "You can try if you like, but it won't do you any good."

"Says you," I said. I reached him with my hands balled up in fists ready to take him out any way I could.

He looked down at my hands. "Fine. Hit me."

"What?" I asked.

"Take a swing. Go ahead."

I thought over the request for a split second and then threw a punch before he had time to change his mind. My fist went right through him. I threw another punch and then another and another. Each time it felt like I was striking cold air. I took a step back on the verge of tears. There was nothing I could do. I turned to the two Billys. I could plead with them to run, but it was obvious they had no idea I was there. The gray man was the only one who could see me.

"We gonna get baseballs, mister?" Billy B asked.

"You bet boys. I got a lot of great surprises in store for you two."

I scrambled to think of what to do. I couldn't stop him, but maybe I could get inside his head. "The older boy saw you."

The old man smiled. "Then I'll have to find him and introduce myself."

"No," I said. "He didn't see anything. Leave him alone."

"You're looking at this all wrong."

It was such a crazy thing to say I would have laughed if I hadn't been so angry and panicked.

"They're just meat."

"They're kids. They've got parents. They're part of a family."

"A calf has a mother. Children on farms think of cattle as

their pets. No one would arrest me if I butchered and ate a calf."

"These are people," I said.

"People are animals, Oz."

My blood boiled. "Never use my name."

He frowned. "We're going to be friends, you know. We're the same. We're bad people."

I couldn't argue. I was bad. I had destroyed the world. I started to back away.

"Don't go," he said. "I'm going to make a delicious stew."

I turned to sprint back to the ladder.

"Stop," he cried. "I'll let you pick one."

I swallowed and said, "Pick one?"

He rolled his eyes. "You can pick one. Do whatever you want with him."

"I don't want to do anything," I said.

"Not even save one?"

My mind nearly split apart just processing what he had just said. Save one. I turned it over and over again in my head, and finally said, "I want to save both of them."

"One or none," he giggled.

"But I can't choose..."

"Fine," he shrugged. "More meat for me."

"Okay," I yelped. "I'll choose... I'll choose."

He smiled. "You have until the count of three."

I looked at the two boys.

"One."

They were so young. They had no idea that they were with a monster.

"Two."

Billy B was three and Billy G was four.

"I say the last number and the deal's off."

"Billy B," I yelled. "Billy B. Billy B."

The old man frowned. "Darn. He's the chubby one. Lot of good fatty meat on that one."

I felt numb. It didn't matter that I had saved Billy B. I had ensured that Billy G was about to die a terrible, tortuous death. "I'm going to find you," I said calmly. "I'm going to find you and torture you. I'm going to make you pay for all this. I'm going to make you feel their pain."

"You see," he said smiling, "we really are alike." With that he knelt down. "Boys, do you know why I brought you up on the roof?"

"A party?" Billy B asked.

"No," the old man said pulling the cover off his tool box. "I brought you up here..." He opened the box and pulled out his favorite knife. "Because I'm the boogeyman!"

DAY 3

FOURTEEN

I woke up leaning against the wall in the back of the closet. Believe it or not, I felt rested, more so than I had since my world ended when I was thirteen. I stretched and yawned and felt something shift on my lap. Instinctively, I reached down to readjust whatever it was. My hand landed on a manila folder labeled "General Estate Maintenance Records: December, 1934." I hadn't remembered pulling it from the filing cabinet. I flipped through the thick folder. None of the contents struck me as particularly important. I was about to close it and never give it another thought when a signature on a form caught my attention. I brought the form closer to my face. It was a bill of sale for paint and, according to the signature, the supervising maintenance director was Nathan Bashir.

Bashir. I processed the information. The name of the doctor in Buffalo who treated Stevie and other patients with Down syndrome was Dr. Bashir... I was almost certain. My mind was a little muddled, but I remembered the name. One of the Destroyers was even named Bashir in honor of Dr. Bashir. Dr. Bashir created the Storytellers. He taught his patients Hyper Mental Imaging, how to create the world around them through intense visualization practices. He taught them... forced them even . . . to get back at those of us who taunted and tortured them. His patients created monsters that crawled out of their imaginations and destroyed the world.

This couldn't be the same Bashir, could it? It was a coincidence. If it was the same guy, he would have been in his nineties when he treated Stevie and the others. Not impossible, but not likely either.

Curiosity got the best of me. I examined the rest of the contents of the folder more closely. It seems there was a significant amount of painting that occurred in the latter part of 1934. More than 100 painters were employed. Lists of hirings and firings filled up a small notebook. I scanned through the names. I came to a sudden stop on the fifth page. Hire number forty-three, Albert Howard Fish.

I unknowingly gripped the edges of the folder more tightly as I soaked in the information. He was here... when he was alive... in this mansion. I hurriedly shuffled through more papers in the folder. Eventually I uncovered something called a "Notice of Termination" with Fish's name on it. The date was December 24, 1934. The name of the person who filled out the form was Nathan Bashir. The reason for termination was scribbled on the page. It was almost impossible to make out. I peered closer and concentrated on each letter. Finally I deciphered it. "Inappropriate behavior around the staff's children."

"No kidding," I whispered to myself.

I flipped the paper over and there was something written on the back. The handwriting matched the chicken scratch on the front.

"Mr. Fish has made inappropriate remarks to many of the children of staff members. He terrified one particular child with stories of a boogeyman who eats the meat of youngsters. This child remarked that Mr. Fish tried to force him off the grounds and into the woods that lay beyond the property. When questioned about these accusations, Mr. Fish grew violent and unruly. Police officers were summoned to escort him to the train station."

The train station? I thought. *Hopefully, they threw him under the train.* They didn't, I know, but I couldn't believe they'd just let him go. They knew what he was. I found other forms in the folder filled out by Bashir, and they were all neatly written. I read those notes with no problem. The termination form was the only form that was barely legible. I read the note to myself a few more times. He was scared, not of Fish. No, he was scared that a man like Fish could even exist. I took the notebook and termination form and put the folder back in the filing cabinet.

I left the closet and walked. I had no idea where I was going. I just walked and considered the new information carefully. We were at this mansion for a reason. The old gray man had some unfinished business here, and we were here to make sure he didn't finish it.

I was standing at the entranceway to the fourth floor observatory room before I knew what hit me. I didn't even recall walking up the stairs. I didn't even remember exiting the bedroom on the second floor.

My stomach knotted up, and I knew Archie and Billy were nearby. Kimball sauntered into the middle of the room and laid down. He was exhausted. I imagine he had stood watch over me while I visited the Land of the Dead.

I was tired, too, but I couldn't rest. I was hungry, and being so close to... meat . . .was driving me crazy. I forgot all about the paper and pen. Leaving Archie and Bobby a note was impossible.

I dropped to one knee and quickly went through the contents of my backpack until I found a long-sleeved shirt. Sitting in a nearby chair, I tied one sleeve to my ankle and the other to a leg of the chair. It wasn't enough to stop me, but it was enough to slow me down.

"I know you're in here," I said. "I can smell you."

Bobby was the first to step out of the darkness. He stood stiff and nervous. "Where's the Flish?"

I shook my head. "I don't know."

Archie stepped out of the same darkness that had concealed Bobby. He was holding the toddler who had once been Tall Boy. "You in bad shape?"

"No," I said. "I'm much worse than that."

"The others?" Archie asked.

"We've all had better days." My mouth began to water just looking at them. I closed my eyes. "We've made a pact."

"Yeah," Archie said, "what kind of pact?"

I snickered. "We're going to give each other space."

My two-way radio screeched and Wes's voice crackled through the small speaker. "Oz? You there? Oz..."

I sighed and clicked to talk. "Go for Oz."

"Where you been, boy? Lou said we were supposed to check in every hour to let everyone know our locations."

I grimaced. "Yeah, I forgot. Got a little sidetracked."

"Pact ain't no good if everybody don't follow the same rules," he answered.

"Couldn't be helped," I said.

"Tell me about the pact," Archie insisted.

I rolled my eyes. "We're going to stay out of each other's way and work on a way to get out of here."

"Flish won't let you leave," Bobby said rolling his eyes at me.

I waved him off. Bobby didn't know me. I could be pretty resourceful when I had to be. I pressed the button and talked to Wes. "I've been to the Land of the Dead, Wes."

There was a long pause before he answered. "Come again."

"The Land of the Dead," I said. "I've been there."

"Must not be all bad," he snickered. "You lived to tell about it."

"It's no picnic," I said. "Listen, the bad guy... The Destroyer, the old guy in the basement, he's based on a real guy... I mean a real guy from our world." I paused to let him talk.

"Go on," he said.

"Albert Fish, he's sick and twisted. Used to kidnap kids and eat them."

"Fish? Albert Fish? I know that name... Yeah," he said excitedly. "Albert Fish. I know him. Know of him anyway. Had an uncle who was obsessed with serial killers. Ol' Albert had his heyday between World War I and World War II, if I remember right."

"What else do you know?" I asked.

"Too much. Uncle used to creep me out with stories about that guy. Fish is the reason New Yorkers started locking their doors."

"He used to write horrible letters to the parents of his victims. Tell them every detail of how their children died. That's how he got caught... Grace," he said at the end of a gasp. "She's the girl. The one in the basement. The one you saw in the second floor bedroom."

"Yeah," I said. "Did you know that Fish was here, in the thirties? He worked as a painter."

There was a pause. "No, but it wouldn't surprise me. He bragged about eating kids in every state. Claims he got four hundred or so of them."

What a grand feast, I thought, and then shook the disgusting idea out of my head. "How could he get away with something like that?"

"Simple," Wes said. "He'd usually kidnap little ones that society didn't want nothing to do with."

"What do you mean?"

"Retarded," I heard little Bobby say.

Wes said, "Kid's like Nate and Stevie and..."

"And the other Storytellers," I interrupted.

"That's right. It was a different time. People would normally institutionalize kids who weren't... normal. Hide 'em away. Fish probably thought he was doing everybody a favor."

I wondered how different it really was. "But Grace wasn't like Stevie and the others."

"I said he usually kidnapped the mentally handicapped. He went off script a few times. That's probably what did him in."

I watched Archie walk across the room bouncing the Throwaway version of his son in his arms. His attitude about the toddler had changed quite a bit. He was holding him like a father holds his son.

I thanked Wes for the information and tossed aside the radio. As soon as I did, I focused my attention on my hunger and the two meals in the room with me.

"So we've got to take down this Flish," Archie said.

"We don't have to," I said. "I do. You, Bobby, and that thing you're holding need to get on the road while it's light out."

"His name is Max," Bobby smiled.

"That's right," Archie said.

I snickered. "Seriously?"

"You got a problem with that?" Archie snapped.

"None of my business," I said.

"You're not a father," he said. "You don't know."

I held my hands up to signal my surrender. "Okay, whatever. If you want to pretend that thing is your son, have at it."

"It's not a thing!" Archie screamed. "My son is not a thing!"

"Don't push me, Archie," I said fighting to keep my calm. If I let go of my anger, one of two things could happen. I could turn full Délon and kill him before he had time to blink, or I could tear his guts out and eat his chewy, delicious insides.

It was his turn to snicker. "Kid, I am older than you and I am Creyshaw. You best not push me."

I gripped the side of the chair and tried to squeeze the frustration out of me. I didn't know if I could hold on much longer.

He grunted and sucked in a big deep breath. He slowly let it out. "We need to be working on this thing together, Oz."

"We can't... it's not safe for you or Bobby. Bobby is all you should be worried about."

He said, "I got news for you. Ain't no such thing as safe in this world. You know that saying 'the devil you know?' Well, brother, you're the devil I know. You and the others. I'll take my chances here. Smart thing for you to do is use me in some way."

I couldn't tell him, but he was right. "Suit yourself," I said untying my leg from the chair. "You want to help. Find out what you can about Albert Fish."

"Sounds like Wes is your man for that."

"He knows some, but I need to know more. I've got seven days to figure him out."

"This Land of the Dead," Archie said. "How do I get there?"

I was about to say that I didn't know when Bobby jumped in.

"Only the dead can go to the Land of the Dead."

I furrowed my brow and shook my head. "But I've been there, and I'm not dead."

Bobby looked away.

I stood up and said it more emphatically. "I'm not dead."

He shrugged. "Dead is dead."

I looked at Archie hoping he would interpret. He was as confused as I was. "What do you mean, Bobby? Oz isn't dead. He's here. He's alive."

"I know," Bobby said as if it was too ridiculous to consider. "But he used to be dead. Once you're dead, you're always dead even if you're alive. That's what Dr. Bashir told us."

"I used to be dead?" I said still trying to understand.

"You got caught in a ripcord," he replied.

"A ripcord?" Archie asked looking at me. This time he wanted me to translate what Bobby was saying.

"A ripcord..." It came to me as the words left my mouth. "Riptide. I got caught in a riptide when I was eleven." The memory came rushing back to me. "I drowned."

"You drowned?" Archie said, still not getting it.

"I died. They revived me on the beach. I was dead." I flopped back down on the chair. "So, I'm the only one who can go to the Land of the Dead..."

"Only the dead can go to the Land of the Dead..." he stopped and turned to Throwaway Max as he cooed. "And the never was. They can go, too."

"That doesn't really help me," I said. "The Throwaways aren't much help."

Bobby shrugged.

"Wait a minute," Archie said moving quickly toward Bobby. "This is a story, isn't it? Like with Carl and the Myrmidons. This is a story."

"It's always a story," Bobby said.

"Then you know what happens?" Archie asked.

Bobby shook his head. "I was too scared to read the whole thing. I didn't like it. Sad stuff happens."

***

We questioned Bobby about the story, but he didn't have much more to offer. He never would say what the sad stuff was, and I couldn't press him on it because the more I did, the more frustrated I got. Frustrated was not a good state for me. I told Archie if he wanted to help, he could get Bobby to spill the beans on everything he knew. It was just too risky for me to stick around, so I radioed in and got everyone else's location. Except Gordy. He wasn't answering, but I really couldn't worry about that.

I was confident no one was in the basement. Gordy wouldn't choose to seclude himself down there. As if I was about to face a firing squad, I slowly made my way down to the main floor with Kimball and stopped in front of the staircase that led down to the basement.

The gray man was down there. He was waiting for me. This was probably his plan all along. Separate us and lure us all down to the basement where he could eat us one by one.

This thought ran through my head as I took the first step and then tumbled all the way down the stairs. I landed with a thud on the floor and heard the sound of metal on metal... like someone was sharpening knives. When I attempted to stand, the world began to spin. I flopped on my back and watched my world turn black.

***

"Detective King," the stout older man said. "Chief Inspector, actually. Manhattan."

The man was introducing himself to a young dark-haired uniformed police officer. "Seen your picture in the paper, Detective King. I'm Officer Roland, Perry Roland."

I was in a police station witnessing the scene like a ghost, just like I always did in The Land of the Dead. The dead boy and I sat on a bench watching the two men talk.

Detective King turned his hat in his hand as he talked. His face was serious and worn. My grandfather would say that he looked as though he was in a never-ending state of unsettled.

"I appreciate you coming all the way to Staten Island, sir," Officer Roland said.

King cleared his throat. "Following every lead I can on this thing. The Budds have become like family to me."

"Yeah, well I know this could be a stretch, but..." The younger officer looked almost embarrassed. "A boy went missing here in '24. Francis McDonnell was his name."

"I remember. I assisted the dental records when they found the body," Detective King said. "You think it has something to do with the Budd case?"

"Not me, sir," the officer said. "The boy's father... he works at this precinct."

"The boy's father is a police officer?" The hardened detective looked like he had just been punched in the stomach.

"Yes, sir, and he won't give up on the idea. He's convinced your Mr. Howard is the same man who took his boy."

"I see," Detective King said in a way that indicated he was highly skeptical. His face said even more. He thought the father was desperate to find answers and grasping at straws.

"The description does match your suspect," Officer Roland said. "Older gentleman, mustache, thin."

"If I remember right, you were looking for a foreigner in this case."

"Yes, sir. Witness saw the boy with a man speaking in a foreign language. Italian, she thought, but she didn't know for sure."

King pursed his lips and picked at some lint on his hat. "Our man's a red-blooded American. No accent, nothing to indicate he's a foreigner."

"I know." The police officer pulled out a small notepad and handed it to Detective King. "I copied this from the case file."

Detective King read what was written on the notepad. "What's this?"

"That's what the witness said she overheard the man saying."

"And?"

"It's not Italian."

"So, she guessed wrong. It's Spanish or German or French or some other language. You should take it to a linguist. Still doesn't have anything to do with the Budd case."

"I did take it to a linguist."

"Good," the detective said putting his hat back on. He was clearly through with this dead end.

"It's not any language."

"Then the witness heard it wrong."

"Maybe," the police officer said. "But this professor I talked to thought it was something else."

"Which is?"

"He thinks the woman overheard our suspect speaking in tongues."

Detective King pushed his hat up and cocked his left eyebrow. "Tongues?"

"Yeah, it's when real religious folks get worked up and start talking in a language that doesn't exist... well, on Earth anyway."

The older detective nodded slowly. "For one who speaks in a tongue does not speak to men but to God; for no one understands, but in *his* spirit he speaks mysteries."

"Sir?"

"From the Bible, Officer Perry. First Corinthians." Detective King was barely participating in the conversation now. He had a faraway look in his eyes. I could almost hear the gears turning in his head.

"Anyway," Officer Perry said. "I got to thinking that you don't have to be a foreigner to speak in tongues. You just got to be super religious. The boy's father might be onto something if that's the case. Your guy be could our guy, too."

Detective King slowly got out of his head and turned to the younger police officer. "He certainly could, Officer Roland. But

I'm afraid that isn't necessarily good news."

The officer looked at the detective perplexed. "Why not, sir?"

"Because if you're right, I am definitely looking for a man who has a history of abducting children. I have a sinking feeling there are many more fathers out there like our fellow officer."

The detective and the uniformed officer shared a few more bits of information before King shook Roland's hand and exited the building. The dead boy and I followed him down the street.

"Any time you want to clue me in on how this Land of the Dead thing works, feel free," I said to my dead companion.

I felt my stomach sink and turn. The young police officer passed through me in a dead sprint.

"Detective King," the officer called out.

The grizzled old cop turned in his direction.

"One last thing," the officer said as he reached the detective.

"I'm listening."

"Your suspect stopped at a newsstand and picked up a package, right?"

The detective nodded. "The newsy said it was a box wrapped in canvas. Howard left it with him before he went to visit the Budds and picked it up with Grace in tow an hour later. Why?"

"Our witness said our suspect had something under his arm. She called it a package, but then changed her mind."

Detective King shut his eyes momentarily and then let out a sigh. "Called it a package? What do you mean?"

The young officer hesitated as if he didn't want to answer the detective's question, but he finally relented. "She called it a package at first, but changed her statement later. The man was dressed like a housepainter, so she assumed it was a small drop cloth folded up and tucked under his arm."

"I see," Detective King said. "But you think it was a package like she originally stated."

Officer Roland shook his head. "It's just an awfully big coincidence, that's all."

King squinted his eyes against the afternoon sun. "Yes, it is, Officer Roland. Yes, it is." The detective got a faraway look in his eyes again.

"What are you thinking, Detective?"

Detective King cleared his throat and said, "I'm just thinking."

"About?"

"What a terrible day it will be when I find out what's in that package."

DAY 4

FIFTEEN

I came to groggy and angry at the bottom of the stairs. I had been to the Land of the Dead three times, and I wasn't any closer to knowing what was going on.

Kimball licked my face as I tried to gather my thoughts. I patted him and gently pushed him away. "I appreciate it, boy, but your breath stinks."

I stood up and worked out the kink in my back. I was getting tired of falling down stairs. It would be nice if my dead pals would put in a door to the Land of the Dead.

My back cracked and popped and I almost felt free of pain. I may have even smiled when I took my first step in a long time without involuntarily groaning. I reached out and placed my hand on the wall. It was cold and rough. It was stone. A stone wall. That's when it hit me. I was in the basement. My mind was in such a haze, I had forgotten where I was headed before my last trip to the Land of the Dead.

It suddenly became difficult for me to breathe. I turned and considered going back up the stairs, but stopped myself as I rested my foot on the first step. I couldn't turn back. Another day had passed. I didn't have time to be scared. "Don't be such a pansy, Griffin," I said. I leaned my head back and yelled, "Get ready, Albert, because I'm coming in!" It was his turn to be a ghost in my world.

Kimball led the way as we moved quickly to the Halloween

room. I stood in the doorway and dashed the flashlight from side to side. I was about to enter feeling relatively sure that there was no one in there, when a shadow seemed to move just outside the limits of the beam of light. I stopped, hesitating before I moved the light back in the shadowy figure's direction. There are some things you're just not sure you want to see. The shadow was gone, but there was something standing in its place... or someone, I should say. I didn't move. I just stared at the cowering figure. He was trembling, but still managed to smile. I opened my mouth to speak, but nothing came out. He was chubbier than I remember him. Kimball approached him with his tail wagging, and the boy who shouldn't have been there reached down and happily patted him on the head.

"I always liked your dog," the boy said.

I gasped at hearing his voice. I could feel the corners of my eyes getting wet. "Stevie?"

***

It seemed as if I stood in the doorway for days without moving, but in reality it was just a few minutes. Seeing Stevie standing there, petting my dog, squinting against the beam of my flashlight, made every hair on my body stand on end. I lost track of time, of myself. Guilt, anger, utter happiness, terror, every emotion you can imagine hit me like bullets from a machine gun.

When I finally moved, it felt like I was walking through syrup. My feet seemed to stick to the floor, and I had to struggle to take each step. I went over a million things to say to him, but all of it seemed stupid. What do you say to the boy you tortured and shamed because he was "slow?" How do you take away the crap you put him through... the crap that led him to take his own life? I'm sorry? That doesn't seem right. I stopped three feet from him and stared at him. He shielded his eyes from the light.

I swallowed the lump in my throat and asked the question I already knew the answer to, "Is this my fault?" I fell to my knees. I wanted him to say no. I wanted him to look at me like it was a ridiculous question, like I was the slow one.

"What?"

I examined his face and saw another beam of light moving in from behind him.

"I thought you weren't supposed to be here, boss," I heard a voice say. It didn't take me long to identify it as belonging to Gordy.

I switched from trying to see Gordy beyond the blinding light to looking at Stevie's face.

"Oz?" Gordy grumbled.

"What," I said as I stood.

"I thought we were supposed to separate."

I was locked on Stevie. "We are."

"This ain't separate, boss man." Gordy dropped the beam of light from my face.

"Didn't know you were down here," I said. "You didn't answer your radio."

Kimball growled, but I didn't pay much attention to it.

"How..." I started, but didn't know how to finish. "Stevie?"

"That?" Gordy giggled. "It's something, ain't it?"

Kimball's growl got louder, but still I didn't notice.

"Not sure why it came out that way," Gordy said.

"Came out that way?"

"Yeah," he said moving closer. "Them Throwaways are freaky."

The air around me suddenly felt lighter. "Throwaway," I said out loud, but to myself. "He's your Throwaway."

Kimball barked. I shined the light on him. His hackles were up, and he was staring holes in Gordy. I moved the light from

Kimball to Gordy, and saw what had my loyal dog aggravated. Gordy was holding an eight inch hunting knife. Before I could tell him to put it down, he leapt for me. I scrambled back, letting go of the flashlight, the beam of light bounced around the room. I heard Gordy land on the concrete floor with a painful crack. He grunted as if he'd had the wind knocked out of him.

Kimball barked and growled. I could hear the tap, tap, tap of his nails on the floor as he rushed Gordy, who still had the knife. I was sure of it because I hadn't heard the clank of the steel blade hitting the floor.

"Get away from me," Gordy squeaked. He was still trying to catch his breath.

I heard Kimball's jaws snap shut, and Gordy let out a terrifying yelp.

"Kimball, stop," I said crawling on my hands and knees to the flashlight. When I placed my hand on it, I heard a swish followed by terrible whine. It was Kimball. I picked up the flashlight and twirled it around the room in the general direction of the commotion. Kimball bared his teeth, but he was moving awkwardly.

Gordy struggled to get to his feet. "You shouldn't have come down here, boss. I didn't want to do it. I didn't want to do it."

"What did you do?" My light glistened off the blade of his knife, and I saw the blood.

"He bit me," Gordy insisted. "What was I supposed to do?"

Kimball was panting heavily now.

"You stabbed Kimball?"

He shook his head. "No, I swear. I just swatted it at him, and I cut him. He's going to be okay. He's going to be okay." Kimball laid down on the floor. "Please be okay, Kimball."

"Drop the knife," I said.

"No way, I need it."

"You don't need it."

"I need it," he yelled. "How else am I going to slice the meat off your bones!"

I should have been creeped out by what he said, but I understood it. Part of me... most of me . . .wanted the knife so I could do the same to him.

Kimball's whining grew more intense.

"We gotta think this through, Gordy. We don't want to eat each other. Not really." I had to hold back a laugh because I really wanted to eat him, and I just sounded ridiculous denying it. "The gray man, he's the one that's doing this to us."

Gordy snickered. "The old man ain't so bad, boss man. He's kind of crazy and babbles on and on, but he kind of reminds me of my grandfather."

"You've talked to him?"

"Can't hardly call it talking, but we've spent some time together."

Throwaway Stevie knelt down beside Kimball and gently stroked his side.

"You shouldn't do that," I said to Gordy.

"Got no choice. He lives in this friggin' basement. The rest of you jerks have taken over the rest of the house. I got nowhere else to go. It's just me and the old man down here. He's harmless, if you want to know the truth. Just talks endlessly about finding his property."

"His property? What property?"

"Got no idea. All he says is it's his, and he needs it. Someone took it from him. 'Had no right to take it,' he says. 'I need the little bits. Can't have the little bits without my property.' It's all he goes on about."

"Your dog needs a band aid," Throwaway Stevie said holding up a bloodstained hand.

I shot Gordy a death glare. I could feel tell-tale signs of the Délon marking rising up inside of me. My blood began to run cold. So cold it burned. I bit my lip and clenched my fists tightly. I couldn't let it take me over. Not now. "If Kimball dies, I swear to you, I will rip you apart and tear the meat from your bones with my bare hands. I won't even need that knife. Do you hear me?"

He looked at Kimball and then back at me. "Yeah."

"Good. Now, let's say we compromise. Give the knife to Stevie."

"That's not really Stevie..."

"You know what I mean," I barked. "Give your Throwaway the knife."

He wasn't happy about the compromise. His eyes darted back and forth from the knife to me. His brain couldn't comprehend not rushing me and just driving the knife into my heart. I just had to hope that there was enough of the Gordy I knew still left in that thick skull of his. Just as I thought there was no way he would do it, he motioned for Throwaway Stevie to take the knife.

Once Stevie had it, I rushed to Kimball's side and examined his wound. He was bleeding pretty badly, but it wasn't as bad as it looked. Gordy had caught him with the blade at the top of his right leg. I wiggled out of my backpack and took out a spare t-shirt to make a bandage.

"Is he okay?" Gordy asked.

I nodded. "Lucky for you, he'll be fine."

***

I sat at the head of a lane of the small bowling alley while Gordy positioned himself by the pins. We kept our flashlights on, but kept them out of each other's faces. Kimball lay at my feet and panted heavily. I gave him what water I had left, but it didn't seem to be enough. I radioed Lou and asked her to send Ajax down with strict instructions that she not come anywhere near the bowling alley. I couldn't look after Kimball and a;sp do whatever it was I needed to do to get us safely out of the mansion and on our way. It was up to my old gorilla friend now to look after both my dog and my... Lou.

"Don't think we're going to make it out of this one, boss," Gordy said. His voice echoed through the large room.

"Yes we are, and stop calling me boss," I answered chasing his echo.

"Feels different," he said.

"How so?"

There was a moment of silence. "I don't want to win this one so much."

"You don't mean that."

He laughed. "If you ain't the boss, you can't tell me how I feel."

"You want to go back home as much as any of us."

"Thought I did, but if you think about it, what am I going back to? My daddy's a mean old drunk. My mom works eighteen hours a day. I spend most of my time trying to avoid getting in trouble for something I didn't do or did without much of a cover up plan. I'm pretty much just as scared back in the real world as I am here, 'cept at least here I get to fight what I'm scared of."

I laughed this time. Not because I thought he was being ridiculous, but because I found myself agreeing with him. We did get to fight back here, and in a lot of ways that made it less scary than it was in the real world. I could see why he didn't want to win.

"I'm telling you, Oz, the old man ain't so bad. You should give him a chance."

I thought about the man I had seen sitting at the Budds' dining room table. He was sinister. I thought about the man on the roof of the apartment building. He was brutal. Gordy didn't know the old man like I did. He knew a babbling old fool looking for his property. "Gordy, you need to stay away from the old man."

"Kind of hard to do when I'm hanging out in his part of the house."

I cringed. I had forgotten that we were in the basement, the place the old gray man called home. I turned to the door that led to the dressing rooms. "He's in there, isn't he?"

"There, here, the other side of the basement. He comes and goes."

I heard a noise to my left and jumped. Throwaway Stevie stepped out of the darkness and started walking towards Gordy. "Didn't know Stevie meant that much to you?"

"He doesn't. Hate the re..." He stopped himself from using the word I hated. "The clown. He started all this."

"We started it," I said. "You know that. Besides you just said you didn't mind it so much."

I could see him tilt his head from side to side. "What do you know? Maybe I don't hate him so much. Anyway, I don't know why my Throwaway came out like this. I was concentrating on a swimsuit model I seen in one of my dad's magazines once."

"Sounds about right," I laughed. "But I don't think it works that way. Somewhere in that empty head of yours, you feel something strong for Stevie."

He waved me off. "I feel nothing for that mush mouth. He did nothing but bug the snot out of me. No matter how bad I treated that idiot, he just kept on coming back for more. Treated me like I was his best friend."

"Me, too."

"He was just too stupid to get lost."

I shook my head. "That's not it."

"What then?"

"He saw the magic in us."

I heard a hoot-bark as Ajax entered from the Halloween room. I stood and turned to him. A silhouette of a girl stood in the doorway. A quick pan of my flashlight revealed Lou.

"I told you not to come," I said to her.

Ajax growled as if to let me know that he was just as annoyed as I was.

"You're not the boss of me," Lou snapped.

"But the pact..."

"I'll stay out of your way. Besides I don't think I have it as bad as the rest of you. I haven't felt like taking a bite out of anyone." She stepped into the room, followed by the Throwaway version of me.

"Him, too?" I groaned. How could she bring him?

Even in the darkness, I could she her cheeks turn rosy red with embarrassment. "I can't help it if he follows me around."

"You told me I could never leave you," the Throwaway said.

"Shut up!" Lou yelled. "I was... that was for you own safety."

Gordy chuckled. "She made her own Oz. How romantic."

"Gordy," I said, trying not raise my voice. "Mind your own business."

Lou saw Kimball lying on the ground and breathing heavily. She couldn't help herself. She ran to his side as quickly as she could. "What happened?"

As she ran by me, I noticed something very odd. I didn't want to eat her. I went over the events of the last few days in my head and tried to remember if I had ever wanted to eat her. I couldn't recall ever being alone with her once the infection started.

She knelt down beside Kimball and started stroking his head. "Oz, what happened?"

"We..." I pointed to Gordy. "We had a misunderstanding.

Kimball tried to help, and he got grazed by a knife. It's not that serious, I just don't have time to look after him and, you know..."

She shook her head. "No, I don't know."

"That's the point," I said. "I don't know either, and I've only got five more days to find out."

"We've only got five more days to find out. You have to stop doing that," she said giving me a disapproving look.

"What?"

"Making it all about you," Gordy chimed in.

"Gordy..." I started, but was quickly cut off by Lou.

"He's right. You're not in this alone."

I growled. She was taking me all wrong. I wasn't saying I was in this by myself. I'm trying to save everyone. Didn't she get that? Besides I didn't see anyone else from our group when I took my little tours of The Land of the Dead. I thought about saying all that to her, but I didn't have the strength or the desire to start a whole thing with her, so I just nodded and apologized.

She smirked because she knew I didn't mean it.

"So, can you and Ajax take care of Kimball?"

Ajax hooted, which I was pretty sure was his way of saying yes.

Much to my dismay, Throwaway me reached down and picked Kimball up. Gordy let out a barrel laugh.

"Stole your girl and your dog, boss man! He takes your job and you got a country song all ready to be wrote!"

Lou stood up and was just inches away from me. I breathed in and got a whiff of her scent. I still didn't want to eat her. For some reason, I wanted to kiss her.

"So, what do you want to do?" she asked.

Her question caught me by surprise. Did she know I wanted to kiss her? I didn't say it out loud, did I? "About what?"

"This place. The goon running around here trying to make

us all eat each other. What are we going to do about it?"

I sighed. She didn't know I wanted to kiss her. She just wanted to know if I had a plan that was going to keep us all from becoming dinner. "I keep going back to the Land of the Dead until I understand what it is I'm supposed to see."

"You've been?"

"Three times."

"And?"

"And besides a lot of bad memories, I got nothing. The old man was a real bad guy in his time."

"What's it like?"

"It's strange. It's not that bad, except for when the old man shows up. It's like olden times. The cars are weird. Everyone's dressed funny. It's the 1920s."

"And you've seen the old man every time?"

I slowly shook my head. "No. Not this last time. I saw these two cops. One was a detective. The other one was in a uniform."

"How do you get there? I should go with you. I mean we don't appear to want to eat each other. You should use me."

I considered it and then said, "You can't go unless you're dead."

"What?"

"Something little Bobby told me. Only the dead and never-was, like the Throwaways, can go to the Land of the Dead."

"You're not dead," she said furrowing her brow.

"I was... it's a long story. Let's just leave it at that." I snapped my fingers. "You could do something else though. Since you don't seem to be... hungry. You can go up to the fourth floor and start grilling Bobby. Ask him everything he knows about the Storyteller who came up with this Destroyer. Why the old man? There's got to be a reason. Some kid with Down syndrome in the 21st century shouldn't even know about a creepy old dude in the 1920s who ate little kids. Something else has to be going on here."

"Okay." She smiled, and I felt better knowing I had her working with me. I pretty much felt like I could do anything with her on my side. I guess she had always been. I just forgot. "Still don't think you should keep going to the Land of the Dead by yourself."

"Not much I can do about that. I don't make the rules."

She motioned toward Throwaway Stevie. "Take him."

I looked him over. "A never was," I said to myself. "Of course." Turning back to her, "You're a genius."

She blushed. "You can have mine, too," she said pointing to Throwaway me.

I almost gasped at the thought. It was just too creepy. "I'll be okay with Stevie."

Her expression quickly changed to surprise. "Stevie? That's 'The' Stevie?"

"Well... no, not really. It's Gordy's version."

She made her way to Throwaway Stevie and looked him over. It was several seconds before she said, "Hello."

Stevie avoided eye contact with her. He looked down and held back an uncomfortable chortle. "Hi."

"It's not really him," I reminded her.

She smiled. "I know, but it's the closest I'll ever come to meeting him.

"I'm glad you're here," Stevie said.

She was a little startled by this statement. Her only reaction was to blush again.

"Do you remember my room?" he asked.

I could feel the chill running up her spine from where I was standing. "Your room?"

"I like my room."

She turned to me, but all I could do was shrug.

"I was in your room once. With Oz. I met your mother. She made us breakfast. How did you know that?"

He squirmed and seemed to grow more and more uncomfortable. He chuckled nervously and pointed to his head. "I have Gordy here."

She stepped back and studied Throwaway Stevie from head to toe. "Gordy, huh?" She leaned in and whispered something in Stevie's ear and then walked back to me.

"What now?" she asked.

I thought it over. "We go our separate ways."

"What about him?" She pointed at Gordy with her thumb.

"What about him?"

"Well, what happens to you when you go to the Land of the Dead?"

"Don't know exactly. I blackout, and I'm just there."

"You're there, but not your body?"

"Near as I can figure."

She folded her arms over her chest. "So, without Kimball, you aren't going to have anybody to watch over the part of you that remains here."

She was right. There would be nothing to stop Gordy from turning me into a meal. "I'll deal with it," I said with no clue as to how I was going to deal with it.

"There you go again," she said shaking her head. "You can't do this alone."

"We don't have a choice. I'll talk to him."

"You two talking about me?" Gordy yelled.

We ignored him.

"Take Ajax," she said.

"No," I responded. I had put Ajax in charge of watching over her. There was no way I was going to leave her alone with a bunch of cannibals running around the mansion.

"Then take you," she said.

"Me?" It took a second or two to figure out she meant the Throwaway version of me. "Not a chance."

She groaned in frustration. "You have to take one."

"I don't..."

"You're taking Ajax."

"No..."

"Look, I know you told him to protect me, but it's not necessary."

I was embarrassed that she knew I had assigned Ajax as her protector. I gave the big ape a dirty look for selling me out. He refused to look at me.

"In case you forgot, I took care of myself and the others while you were gone. I'm not a little girl anymore."

"It's out of the question..."

She cut me off. "Save it." Turning to Ajax she signed something to him and then directed Throwaway me to follow her.

"What did you tell Ajax?" I asked.

She smiled. "I told him not to let anything happen to you. He's your protector now."

"Lou," I protested.

She held up her hand to shut me up as she back-peddled toward the Halloween room. "It's time for you to be a warrior, not a hero."

***

I stepped into a dressing room with Throwaway Stevie while Ajax stood guard outside. I kwew Gordy couldn't make his way past the big ape, but I was still a little concerned about the Flish. As far as I knew, he could walk through walls and go anywhere he pleased, but it was a chance I was going to have to take.

Stevie sat on a chair in the corner of the small room. I plopped down on the floor.

"Are we going home?" Stevie asked.

"Someday," I said.

"What are we doing?"

"Waiting."

"For what?"

I sighed. "Something." Truth was I had no control over my trips to The Land of the Dead. They just snuck up on me. I wasn't even sure how I was going to get Stevie there with me. I was trying to figure out a way to explain this to him when I felt the floor shake beneath me. It was a gentle rocking at first, but it quickly grew more and more violent.

"What's wrong?" Stevie said grabbing onto my forearm.

"Nothing to worry about," I said. "We're just taking a little..." The shaking suddenly stopped. "... trip."

Throwaway Stevie looked awestruck by the experience. His chest was expanding and contracting from his labored breathing.

"Calm down," I said.

"Where are we?" he asked.

Confused I said, "We're here... nowhere... we didn't go anywhere." And we hadn't. We were in the small dressing compartment. Nothing had changed. Or had it? It did seem a little brighter. I stood up and pushed the door to the small room open. Light poured in.

"This isn't here," Stevie said.

I shielded my eyes from the almost searing light. "No... it's definitely not here." My eyes adjusted and I could see that we were now standing on a busy sidewalk. We were no longer in the same place or the same time. We were in the Land of the Dead. The way the people dressed, along with the appearance of the dead boy, told me that.

"What are we doing here?" Stevie asked.

"I wish I knew."

The dead boy started to walk away. I instinctively started to follow him, but Throwaway Stevie didn't move. I motioned for him to come along, but he didn't budge.

"We've got to go with him," I said.

Stevie slowly shook his head.

"He has something to show us."

"I don't want to see it," he said looking as scared as I had ever seen anyone look.

I smiled. "I know how you feel, but it's important." I stuck my hand out for him to grab onto. He examined it and then took hold of it. I pulled him to his feet and we followed the boy.

Stevie flinched every time someone passed us on the street. "They don't feel right."

"Try to ignore them," I said. "They can't see you."

He fixed on a spot ahead of us and pointed. "He can."

He was pointing to the gray man. It was a younger version of him, but it was definitely him. He grimaced when he saw us approach, but he was clearly agitated before he even saw us. He was pacing in a small circle and gnawing on his fingernails.

"It wasn't hers to sell," he mumbled. "I have to get it back."

The sign above the shop where he was standing read, "Patterson Pawn."

"It's mine. It's mine. It's mine."

There was a note on the door of the pawn shop that said the owner was shutting down for a few days due to a family wedding.

"Have to get it back. It's mine." Even though the old man was younger on this visit to the Land of the Dead, he looked weaker, more unsure of himself, than he had on previous trips. One thing was certain, he really wanted something that was in that pawn shop.

"Problem?" I asked.

He jumped at the sound of my voice, and it made me feel really good. He was scared of me.

"What's wrong?"

"Don't talk to me," he begged. "Please."

I giggled. "Oh, this is fun. The big bad boogeyman is afraid of little old me."

He cowered as I moved in closer. "Yes, I'm afraid. I'm afraid. I'm afraid."

I looked at the dead boy. "You finally made this worth my while."

The dead boy motioned for me to look inside the pawnshop, but I was enjoying myself too much.

"Listen to me, old man, you go anywhere near any kids, I will haunt the crap out of you."

"They need me. I do them good. I save the kids, but I can't anymore. She gave it away. She sold it. It wasn't hers, but she sold it."

"Who sold what?"

"She sold it. My fat ugly wife. She sold what's mine and left with that man."

I couldn't believe my ears. "You had a wife? You mean someone actually married you?"

The dead boy grabbed my hand and tugged.

"What?" I asked, irritated that he would interrupt my fun.

Again he motioned for me to look inside the shop.

I groaned and did as he asked, but not before I raised my fist and pretended I was going to throw a punch the old man's way. He had the reaction I had hoped. He whimpered and covered his head with his arms.

I looked inside the pawnshop window through cupped hands It took me awhile to spot what the dead boy wanted me to see, but when I did, it made sense to me. On the back shelf behind the counter was the old man's canvas-wrapped package.

I turned to the old man. "She sold your package. She knows what you are."

"She had no right. I have to save the children. I need my package to save the children."

"Save the children? You call what you do saving the children?"

"It's mine. It's mine. It's mine," he repeated over and over again.

I stepped toward him, but stopped when I noticed Throwaway Stevie staring a hole in me. "What's with you?"

"I'm just trying to see it."

I raised an eyebrow. "See what?"

"It. The magic."

I raised both eyebrows. "What?"

"She said there was magic in you."

"Who said?"

"Lou. In the basement."

"What?"

"She whispered in my ear about your magic."

"She whispered in your ear..."

"Yeah," he said excitedly. "She said 'You were right to choose Oz. There really is magic in him.'" He hesitated and said, "What did I choose you for?"

"I'm not sure," I said.

The old man growled. "She had no right!"

Stevie looked at him and then back at me. "Maybe you can use your magic to get his property for him?"

The Land of the Dead went completely silent. The people on the streets vanished in the blink of an eye. It was just me, the old man, and Throwaway Stevie, whose words still hung in the air. *His property.*

DAY 5

SIXTEEN

An echoing roar stirred me out of my sleep or whatever state you call it when you go to the Land of the Dead. I sat up with a jolt and had to wait a few seconds for my eyes to adjust to the extreme darkness. I felt around for my flashlight, found it, and clicked it on. I was back in the small dressing compartment.

Another roar.

I twirled around. Where was Throwaway Stevie?

A scream.

I threw my shoulder into the door to the dressing room and headed for the bowling alley. The commotion was in full swing. There was a thunderous roar followed by another. The beam of my flashlight zoomed across two furry animals pounding on each other. It was hard to make out what was going on in the sliver of light, but as soon as I saw the silver hair on the backs of both animals, I knew what was going on. Ariabod and Ajax were involved in a knockdown, drag out brawl.

"Hey!" I shouted.

They ignored me and continued to pound away on each other.

"Stop!"

They rolled on the floor in a tangled mess. I couldn't tell one from the other.

A scream came from behind me. I turned to see Gordy on top of April, his knees pinning her arms to the floor. She was snapping her jaws like a wild animal. He was holding his injured shoulder.

Gordy laughed a horrible, maniacal laugh. "You bit me! It's my turn now!"

I started trembling with anticipation. He was going to eat April. I couldn't wait to see. I couldn't wait to taste. I inched towards them, the light from my flashlight bouncing as I walked. The beam fell on the faces of Throwaway Stevie and June huddled together just beyond Gordy and April. They were terrified. The looks on their faces snapped me out of my bloodlust and hunger.

I barreled across the room and grabbed Gordy by the back of his collar. He reached up and tried to slap my hand away. His knees lifted off of April's arms enough for her to work them loose. She shifted and maneuvered her head next to his calf and bit down, sending Gordy into a shrieking frenzy. He twitched and bucked like a mad man until he worked himself free of my grip and jerked back, pulling his leg away from April. I could hear his flesh tear from his calf. It sounded as if someone was ripping a plastic bag open.

The cry Gordy let out at that point was as loud as anything I had ever heard. He clutched his leg and writhed on the floor. April was chewing away on the piece of flesh she had bitten off Gordy's leg. Blood was dripping from the corners of her mouth and was smeared across her chin. My stomach burned. I wanted a taste so badly.

Meanwhile, Ajax and Ariabod were still going at it. I grabbed April by her hair and yanked her to her feet. She yelped in pain.

"You're coming with me," I said.

She fought me as I dragged her towards the two gorillas. I got as close to them as I dared and hollered as loud as I could, "Help!"

That stopped them. Their instinct to save a human in distress was greater than their desire to kill each other. They both looked at me panting and wide-eyed.

"Now, I get why frick and frack were going at it, but what is up with you two?"

Ajax began to sign, but I waved him off. "Don't bother. I only know a few signs. I'd need Lou to translate."

"I can tell you what happened," April said.

I still had her by her hair. One look at her and I could see that I was dealing with somebody who was completely out of her mind. I slowly loosened my grip and backed away from her.

She started licking her fingers like she had just eaten a greasy drumstick. "I broke the pact."

"You what?"

"I took a bite out of the king of the jerks over there and gorilla 'A' tried to break me in half. Gorilla 'B' came to my rescue."

Gorilla 'A' was Ariabod. "You were going to kill her?"

April was licking up as much of the blood on her chin as she could reach with her tongue. She took time out to defend Ariabod. "He was only doing what he was asked to do. Something Chicken-Little gorilla was too wimpy to do."

"Chicken-Little just saved your life."

"And allowed me to get a second bite, thank you very much," she said taking a bow.

I shook my head. "Ajax, next time let Ariabod kill her." I didn't mean it. At least I don't think I meant it. It was hard to think straight with the smell of human blood so strong in the room.

Gordy continued to moan. She had taken a big chunk out of his leg, and I didn't think he was going to recover any time soon.

April smiled and I could see a piece of skin hanging from her teeth. "Oh, man that was so yummy." She started for Gordy, but I pushed her back.

"Not a chance," I said pushing her toward Ariabod. "Hold

onto her. Don't kill her."

He growled.

I took one step toward Gordy, but stopped. I could smell his open wounds from where I was standing. They were mouthwatering. I imagined myself sinking my teeth into the open wound on his calf and tearing the tender muscle from the bone. It was sweet and savory. I couldn't imagine anything that could taste better.

Sensing what was on my mind, Gordy demanded that I not get near him. He clutched his calf with both hands and did his best to stop the bleeding. His shoulder was bleeding, too, but he didn't appear to be as concerned about that injury.

I heard a cackle over my left shoulder and wheeled around to see the old gray man hovering near the doorway to the dressing room area.

"Soup's on," he screeched.

Ajax growl-hooted but didn't advance.

The Flish flashed an awful yellow grin at me. "Go on, young pup. Have your breakfast. I'll be having mine soon enough."

I wanted to step towards him, but I couldn't bring myself to do it. I knew he couldn't hurt me... rather, I was pretty sure he couldn't hurt me, but still, I couldn't work up the courage to confront him, not here, not like I could in the Land of the Dead.

"Not if I have anything to do with it," I said.

He giggled. "Time's running, my boy. I'll have what's mine soon enough."

The word 'mine' triggered the memory of my latest trip to the Land of the Dead. He was terrified and panicked because he didn't have his package. "Your property?" I asked.

His face lit up. "That's right. My property. Do you know where it is? Give it to me."

I had him. He needed that package. I didn't know why or for

what, but he needed it, and as long as he thought I knew where it was, maybe I could use it to my advantage. "I know where it is," I said hoping he couldn't read lies.

He lumbered towards me which didn't make Ajax happy. Ajax roared and moved between me and the old man.

"Give me my property!" the old man insisted.

"Ask me nicely," I said.

The old man ground his teeth. I said, "Give me my property!" He kept coming in spite of Ajax blocking his way.

"It's mine now!" I yelled.

The Flish picked up the pace. Ajax roared! The old man ignored him.

"It's mine! You have no right! The children need me!"

Ajax charged the Flish and plowed into him with a powerful thud. The old man disintegrated on impact.

"Whoa!" I barked.

Ajax twirled around looking for the Flish, but he was nowhere to be found.

Gordy managed to sit up. His head darted from left to right. "He's not gone."

"I know," I said. "I feel him." I zoomed the flashlight around looking for the creepy old ghost.

"Give him his property," April screamed. She was trying to work herself free from Ariabod's grip.

"It's not his any more," I said. "It's mine."

A wail echoed through the long room, and we could hear running feet, but it was impossible to tell which direction they were coming from.

"Did you hear me?" I asked. "It's my property now!"

"Nice going," Gordy said. "That's not helping."

"I know what I'm doing..." the words no sooner left my mouth than I heard a horrible hiss as I was pushed to the ground. The old man's stinking hot breath struck me in the face as his knees jammed into my chest. His dingy yellow teeth glistened as the old man snarled. "It's mine. You have no right." I struggled to get him off me. Ajax roared and the old man groaned with frustration. "You'll pay for this."

With that, he was gone.

***

I radioed Lou and asked her to come to the basement without Kimball and the Throwaway version of me. They could stay with Archie and Bobby.

She still wasn't feeling the effects of the Flish, which meant that she was in less danger than any of us, which also meant that she was going to have to be the go between for all of us until we either figured out a way to lift this curse or ran out of time and ate each other.

She cleaned and dressed Gordy's wounds. He moaned and complained the whole time. He wanted to know why he was the one who always got injured.

"Karma," Lou answered.

"I don't even know what that is," Gordy replied.

"Means you should try to be nicer in the future," she said.

"Good luck with that," I said sarcastically, standing about ten feet away.

"It could happen," Lou said.

"No," Gordy said. "He's right. It's probably not going to happen."

"Let me go!" April shouted. Ariabod still had a tight grip on her. I sensed that he was really confused as to why I wouldn't let him kill April. After all, she had broken the pact by taking a bite out of Gordy.

Lou stood. "What are you going to do with her?"

I thought it over. "I'd put her with you, but I need you to be able move freely among us. She would complicate things for you."

Lou agreed. "Lock her up."

"What?" I asked.

"Put her in jail until we figure this thing out."

"Jail?"

"Saw a utility closet in the Halloween room with a key hanging on a hook next to it. Lock her in the closet and give me the key. That way no one can get to her and she can't get out and take a bite out of anyone else."

"No, no," April said. "You're not locking me in a closet."

I smiled at Lou. It was brilliant. "Actually, we are," I said.

"That's not fair!" April yelled. "How come no one else has to be locked in a closet?"

"Karma," Gordy yelled back. He looked at Lou. "Right?"

She walked toward the Halloween room with Ariabod dragging April along. "Basically."

***

"So," I said talking to Lou in the stone-walled hallway. "What did Bobby have to say?"

She rolled her eyes. "What didn't he say? It's hard to get him to shut up once you get him started."

"About Fish's Storyteller? Did you get anything from him about that?"

She smiled. "Connie Robbins. She was the youngest in the group."

"Did Bobby know her?"

She crossed her fingers and held them up. "They were like this. Bobby couldn't really cross his fingers, but I'm pretty sure that's what he meant."

I waited for her to elaborate, but she didn't.

"And?"

She shook her head and rubbed her brow. "Oh, sorry. It's just a little confusing. I talked about it with... you know... you early this morning," she pointed up.

"Me?

"Not you," she said sounding frustrated. "The other you. The Throwaway you. He and I talked. I'm all turned around." She thumped her head with her index finger.

I was disturbed to hear that she had confused me with the Throwaway version of me. I got angry that he was having my conversations with her.

"Connie was only the second girl in the group," Lou said. "One of Dr. Bashir's favorites. Took her longer to master the Hyper Mental Imaging. She didn't like to draw, so she kept a journal."

"A journal?"

"Well, an HMI journal. She didn't write what really happened. She wrote what she wanted to happen. Same principle as the comic books, but without pictures."

"Why Fish?"

"That's a little unclear. Bobby didn't think it was her idea. She didn't like making up monsters. Didn't have it in her."

"Who gave her the idea?"

"Well," Lou said. "That's what we... Throwaway you and I were talking about this morning. It's got to be Bashir. Like you said, what are the chances she'd know about this creep? He had to plant this stuff in her head, which kind of confirms what I already thought about Bashir."

I wanted to cringe at the notion that she talked to Throwaway me about this already, but I didn't. "Which is?"

"He's not a nice guy. I mean Bobby already told us he hit some of the members in the group, but this takes things to a whole new level. He planted a real life monster in Connie's head. What kind of sick freak would do that?"

"One we need to find out more about," I said. I told her about the Nathan Bashir who used to work at the mansion in the '30s. It was too much of a coincidence. There had to be a connection.

"Can't be the same guy," she said.

"Maybe not the same guy, but it might be the same family." I told her about Fish's time at the mansion, the termination form, and the notes written by a man named Bashir.

"So, what do you think?" she asked. "This is all because Fish did something to a relative of Dr. Bashir?"

"I don't know what to think. I'm just trying to talk it out." I smiled. "It actually feels good to have someone to talk to that I don't want to... you know, eat."

She bowed her head. "I'm honored."

"Not sure why you didn't get infected by Fish, but I'm glad you didn't."

She nodded but her brow furrowed, and she tried to hide it from me.

"What?"

"Nothing," she said.

"No, come on. Something's bothering you."

She rolled her eyes as if to warn me she was about to say something really crazy. "Why wasn't I infected?"

Not knowing what to say, I just blurted out, "Because you're stronger than the rest of us."

"Stronger?"

"Inside," I said. "You've got will power or faith or conviction or something like that."

She considered my theory and then said, "That explains why I don't want to eat you guys, but how come you guys don't want to eat me?"

"Who cares?" I asked. "Stop looking a gift horse in the mouth."

She cleared her throat. "I just know nothing's free around here."

"Don't worry," I said. "I'll make sure nothing happens to you."

"You will?"

"Well, all of us," I said nervously. "The others, too."

There was a second of uncomfortable silence between us. She broke it by asking, "What next?"

"We still need to know more from Bobby. Tarek said the Flish consumed the Creyshaw, but we still don't know anything about the Keeper. And, what does Fish's package have to do with this?"

"Package?"

"His property. It's a metal box wrapped in a canvas cloth."

"What's in it?"

I hesitated. "Knives, bone saw. Run of the mill tools of torture."

"Nice," she groaned and took a step back towards the Halloween room.

"Hey," I said.

She stopped and looked at me. "Yeah?"

"If day nine comes around, and we're no closer to solving this thing, you need to leave with Archie and Bobby. Take the gorillas and Kimball, too."

She stared at me stone-faced.

"I need to hear you say you'll leave."

"It won't come to that."

"It might," I said. "And Bobby is the priority. Tarek will put up a fight, but you can wear him down. He'll take Bobby and stand in for his Keeper."

She started to walk away again, but I grabbed her by the arm. "Say it."

She hung her head. "I'll take care of it."

"You'll leave?"

"Yes, I'll leave. Happy?"

"No," I said letting her go. "But I'm satisfied."

***

Lou checked on Gordy one last time before she left the basement. I hated to see her go. Beyond being the only person I knew that I didn't want to eat, I just felt better around her. I had been away from her for a long time living in the facility. Now I was under the same roof with her, but the Flish was keeping us apart. It was almost too much to take.

I was in a crazy, twisted world, full of all kinds of bad guys and monsters fighting for my life, but if it wasn't for this world, I would never have met Lou. That made it hard to completely hate the way things had turned out. I suppose it's bad for me to say, but if I hadn't treated Stevie so badly, I wouldn't know Lou at all. I never would have known how good she smells or how her nose twitches like a rabbit when she laughs. I wouldn't have known that there was someone I could count on one hundred percent of the time.

"What are you thinking about, boss man?" Gordy asked from the other side of the room. He was propped up on one elbow, sipping from a bottle of water. With Ajax and Ariabod in close proximity, there was no danger of us trying to eat each other. Even if they weren't around, there was no chance he was coming after me. He couldn't move after what April did to him. His face was getting puffy. I had seen my aunt in the hospital after she had a car accident. Her face had the same kind of red and swollen look that Gordy's face had. I remember a nurse saying something about antibodies and infection. Whatever that meant, it looked like Gordy had the same thing.

"I thought I told you not to call me that?"

"Did you?" His eyes rolled to the left as he tried to remember that conversation. "I'll stop then. Don't know why you don't like it anyway?"

"Because I'm not your boss man."

He nodded. "You're right, you're not my boss man."

I half smiled to thank him for the confirmation.

"You're THE boss man. The big cheese. The man with the plan."

"Shut up or I'll let April out of the closet."

He chuckled. "Let her out. What do I care? Better yet, I'll give you the first bite. Come on over here. I hear the rump is the best part."

My stomach practically roared at the thought. I very much wanted to take him up on his offer. I envied April for getting to rip off a chunk of meat and eat it. "I'll pass," I struggled to say.

A few seconds passed before either one of us spoke again. The theme of the conversation had become too tempting, and both of us seemed to know not to push our luck.

"You never did tell me what you were thinking?"

"What?"

"You had what my dad used to call a Mars face. As in, you were on a different planet there for a second. What's up?"

"What's not up?" I asked with a yawn.

"True, but you looked like you had something specific on your mind."

"No..."

"It's Lou, ain't it?"

I went slack jawed. How did he know?

"You're wondering the same thing I am."

"Which is?"

"Why isn't she infected by the old man?"

"You're wondering that?" I asked perplexed.

"Sure. You're not?"

I shook my head. "She's immune."

"I got a theory," he said. "You want to hear it?"

"I don't know. Do I?"

"C'mon, I'm pretty proud of myself for coming up with it."

I sighed. "Okay, go ahead."

"Well," he said "I figure she's dead."

The world slowed to a crawl. I could hear every breath I took. The vein in my neck began to throb. I felt the world dim like I was about to pass out, but I snapped myself back to the present. "You figured wrong," I said just above a whisper.

"Hear me out," he said. "The old guy, he ain't got much use for the dead. You should hear the way he talks about your dead friend and the other little buggers running around here. He hates them. Doesn't want anything to do with them. Lou must be dead. It's the only thing that makes sense."

"Dead people don't..." I stopped myself before I said something I knew wasn't true, but he knew exactly what I was going to say.

"Dead people don't walk around, talk to you like nothing's wrong? You forget where we are, my friend. This is the end of the friggin' world. There's dead people all around us."

"Not Lou," my voice was louder. I could feel the ice moving through my veins. The Délon in me wanted out, but Gordy was clueless. He pushed the issue.

"Ten bucks says she's in one of them rooms upstairs, half the meat stripped from her bones. I can even guess who caught her and is eating her. Want to know who?"

"Stop," I growled.

Ajax hooted at me while he knuckle-walked in our direction. If he could talk, he would be telling me to settle down and get a hold of myself.

"Wes. That fat redneck is having him a regular Lou picnic right now. I know it as sure as I know you want to kill me right now."

I looked at my hands. They were covered with purple blotches. It was happening. "I am going to kill you."

"Good," he yelled. "Do it!"

I pounded the floor with my fist and wasn't surprised when the solid surface crumbled from the blow. If I wanted to eat him, why didn't I? What was holding me back? Why did I value human life so much? It seemed ridiculous. I stood with every intention of ripping the flesh from his bones, but I was knocked to the ground before I could take a step.

"Let him go," Gordy cried. "Let him do it!"

I stared into the grimacing face of Ajax. He was huffing and howling and doing everything in his power without actually touching me to keep me from charging Gordy. He didn't want to physically restrain me because he understood that would just frustrate me more and drive me even further into a Délon frenzy. The others didn't know how lucky they were. They only had to deal with being possessed by the old man. I was dealing with two demons inside of me.

"Get out of his way, you big dumb ape. I want this!"

I paced in half circles in front of Ajax and fought to suppress all the evil that was trying to take hold of me. I started repeating my name over and over again. I just had to remind myself who I was.

"I can't take this any more," he shouted. "Don't you understand? I'm begging you to put me out of my misery."

Ariabod sauntered over to Gordy and sat on his haunches next to him. His massive head turned from me and back to Gordy three or four times. He flashed a gnarled grin. Gordy wouldn't shut up, and I was growing more and more agitated by the minute. Ariabod scooted around and put his butt to Gordy's face. He nodded his massive head several times. Ajax grinned and nodded back. Ariabod leaned forward and passed gas... loudly.

I was startled. My mouth fell open as I stared in disbelief at what he had just done.

Gordy screamed as if he'd been lit on fire. "He farted! He farted!"

I burst out laughing. It was completely absurd. I had been on the verge of tearing Gordy limb from limb. Gordy was begging me to kill him. I was going mad with frustration. In an instant, the frustration was gone. I was laughing like I had not laughed in years. My belly started to ache I was laughing so hard.

"Oh my God!" Gordy said, crawling away backwards. "A huge friggin' gorilla just farted on me."

I held on to my sides and bent over. "That is the funniest thing I've ever seen."

"Funny? I smell like gorilla fart now!"

"You should have seen your face," I said.

Gordy looked surprised that I was enjoying myself so much. He frowned, but I could see him fighting a smile.

"It's not funny."

"It is totally funny," I said between waves of snorting laughter.

He couldn't hold it back any longer. He slapped the floor and started laughing along with me. "That was so sick," he screamed.

Ariabod and Ajax hoot-laughed along with us. Throwaway Stevie and June looked on confused but pleased that we were so thoroughly enjoying ourselves.

Just like that, Ariabod had defused the situation. I went from wanting to kill Gordy to laughing my guts out. Gordy went from wanting to die and antagonizing me to joining me in a good solid laugh.

I fell to the floor and started to get myself under control. I dabbed at my eyes as tears of laughter fell. "Man," I said. "I needed that."

Gordy sighed. "You weren't on my end."

I breathed in deeply and blew out a long stream of air. "You can't do that again, Gordy."

"It wasn't me. It was the big ugly gorilla."

"I don't mean that. I mean you can't provoke me like you did. I was this close, man..."

He thought about what I said. "I'm sorry, Oz."

I looked at him puzzled. He rarely apologized, and when he did, he usually followed it up with something that completely invalidated his apology.

"I'm not a very good friend."

I gave him a look of sympathy. "Stop it."

"It's true, and I'm not just talking about now. I haven't been a good friend for a long time. I kind of feel like you were the way you were with Stevie because of me."

I waved him off. "Let's not get into it."

"My dad called me an instigator. I just love starting trouble. I was the one who always pushed you to be a rat to Stevie, and look where it's gotten us."

I wish I could have blamed him, but I couldn't. I was responsible. He played a part, but I'm the one who made this happen. I was the reason we were here. Not because Stevie was mad at me, but because he wanted me to find the magic in me.

***

Evening came and I went to the pool with Ajax, Throwaway

Stevie, and Throwaway June. Gordy was looking worse by the hour so I left Ariabod behind to watch over him. April was still locked in the closet, and I didn't think she could get out, but I no longer trusted the others to keep the pact. I wasn't sure how I was able to keep it. I couldn't eat my power bars any more. I had taken one bite earlier in the day and immediately spit it out because it made me want to vomit. That was the old man's plan now. He was going to make it impossible for us to eat anything except each other. By my count, we had four more days to go until our nine days were up. I didn't think there was any way we could make it. I had to find the answer soon.

We all gathered on the floor of the empty pool. I leaned against the side and stretched out with Throwaway June and Stevie on either side of me. Ajax sat and watched from the foot of the ladder leading down to the bottom of the pool.

By now, I was used to these little trips to the Land of the Dead, and I was able to relax. Unfortunately, my two Throwaway buddies weren't so lucky. They were nervous and unsure. Their breathing was shallow and loud. It didn't help that we were sitting in a huge cavernous pool that amplified every little sound.

I wasn't even sure why I was taking them with me, but something in my gut told me I should. The dead boy didn't seem to mind that Stevie was with me last time, so why not bring them? Experiencing the old gray man in his world by myself was not the most fun I've ever had. I suppose having company just seemed like a nice thing.

"I don't think I should leave April," Throwaway June said.

I picked at a loose tile on the floor. "April's not April anymore."

"She changed?" Throwaway June asked.

"Yep," I said. "We all have."

"Like us," she said.

"What do you mean?"

"The Throwaways, we changed. First we were nothing, and now we are like you."

I thought about what she said. "Looking like us doesn't make you like us."

She smiled. "What would make us like you?"

"Doing something on your own. Stop watching and be part of the story."

Before I could answer, I heard a small crash at the deep end of the pool followed by a clank, and another clank, and then a rapid series of clanks. It was as if it was raining marbles.

I stood and instructed Throw-away June and Stevie to come with me. "I think our ride's here," I said.

They held on to each other, and we approached the source of the sound at a snail's pace. Through the darkness, I could see the tile and plaster on the side of the pool falling away. A hole the size of a door was slowly taking shape. A face appeared in the darkness through the hole, and I could see that it was the dead boy. I motioned for my guests to hurry. After several seconds of coaxing, I got Throwaway June and Stevie to follow me through the hole.

***

Stepping through the darkness, we found ourselves on an old-fashioned trolley car. Although I guess it was really a new-fashioned trolley car in the Land of the Dead. The car was about half-full. None of the passengers saw us, of course. We stood in the back of the trolley and watched the passengers intently. I had never thought about it on any of my other trips to the Land of the Dead, but it occurred to me that all these people were dead. They ceased to breathe, to go to work, to talk with their friends and family. They were just no more. It was the exact opposite of my situation. I lived in the world where I breathed, but my friends and family (most of them) were gone. They were just no more. I didn't know who was better off, me or the people on the trolley.

The car came to a stop and several people got off, and an even bigger group boarded. They filed on and took their seats. I almost didn't notice the last two. It was the old man and Grace. I clenched my teeth as I watched him shower the little girl with attention. He giggled and asked her about her dress and patted her head. I couldn't take it. I walked over to them and stood in front of the monster. He nonchalantly placed his package on the seat next to him. I went wide-eyed. Oh, if I could just grab it and walk it out of the Land of the Dead. That would be the end of this. I knew it. The old gray man would be useless without his property.

The old man pretended not to see me. I knew he could. Every once in a while he stole a quick glance at me and then quickly looked away. He saw me, but he didn't want to startle the girl so he played it cool.

"I'm going to win, old man," I said.

He twitched, but did not take his eyes off Grace.

"I can't stop you from what you're about to do to Grace, but I can make you pay. It might take me a million years, but I promise you I will find a way to make you pay for everything that you've done."

He snickered involuntarily. A bubble of snot came out of his nose, and he quickly reached up and wiped it away with the back of his hand. His lip trembled.

"I know you're dead. I'm not talking about that. I'm talking about making your insides pay, your soul. I don't know how it works, but I'll figure it out. That's what I do. I figure things out."

He reached out and pinched Grace's cheek. "Look at those tasty little cheeks." He looked at me from the corner of his eye and sneered. "My niece is going to have such a good time with you. She'll be so excited to have a new friend..." he turned to me and looked me dead in the eye, "for dinner."

The trolley stopped, and he grabbed Grace's hand and jumped in line with a group of people exiting. He stood inches from me and, as he headed for the door, he tipped his hat to me.

I groaned and balled my hands into fists. *Just one punch*, I thought. *Give me just one.* I looked down at the seat next to the one he'd been sitting in, and there it was, his package. He had forgotten about it. He took a step toward the exit and looked back at me. I stepped between him and his view of the canvas-wrapped box. He took another step, towing little Grace behind him. He was going to forget it. He was going to step off the trolley without it, and the trolley would pull away with his precious property on board. I held back a smile as he reached the door. He gave me one last look and then stepped down onto the street, extending his hand to help little Grace off.

"Go," I whispered. "Just go."

Grace reached out for his hand and then recoiled. I smiled. She knew. She sensed it. Maybe this didn't have to turn out the way it did in real life.

"Grace, dear, what's wrong?" Fish asked.

"Wait," she said running back towards me. I was astonished. Could she see me? Was she coming to me for help?

She stopped right in front of me, looked down, and grabbed the package. She ran back to the door yelling, "You forgot your package!"

The old gray man grew a hideous grin as she handed the canvas-wrapped box to him through the trolley door. He glanced at me through the window and winked. He and Grace began their trek to the horrible, horrible end that awaited her. It almost hurt too much to think about. She was going to die because she reminded the devil that he had forgotten his tools of terror.

DAY 6

SEVENTEEN

I couldn't risk checking on Gordy. I was really hungry, and I could smell his wounds the minute I climbed out of the pool. I instructed Throwaway Stevie to join him and help Ariabod watch him. I then gave Throwaway June the option to go with him. But she asked if she could go with me.

"I thought you'd want to be close to April."

"She is not April any more."

I smiled and agreed to let her come with Ajax and me. I actually didn't mind at all. I was looking forward to the company, even if it was only Throwaway company.

Passing the door to the dressing room, I paused as we parted with Throwaway Stevie. I thought long and hard about giving in to my urges. Eating Gordy wasn't something I just desired to do, it seemed essential to my survival. I gave myself reasons to do it. I was the key to bringing the old world back. Everybody thought so. Didn't I owe it to everyone to survive? Eating Gordy gave me the best chance to make it out of here and make sure we all had a home to go back to... well, everyone except Gordy.

Ajax, reading my mind, sat in the doorframe making sure I couldn't pass. I hated him for it. We made our way through the basement to another staircase located next to what looked like a laundry room. The stairs took us to a part of the first floor that was not familiar to me. The walls seemed to be soaked in the smell of tobacco. We crossed into a room with a dusty old pool table. I never really played the game, but seeing the table made me wish I had played. Back in the good old days when I didn't want to eat my friends, and I wasn't spending my days trying to figure out how to save the world that I had destroyed.

I ran my hand across the smooth felt surface of the table. It felt familiar even though I didn't play. It was just part of the world I knew, the world I wanted back.

"Play?" I heard a rough and gravelly voice ask.

I looked down at the end of the table and saw Wes sitting in the far, right corner, half cloaked by the darkness. I should have smelled him before I saw him, but the tobacco odor was too strong. Seeing him, my stomach gurgled and burned. He grabbed his stomach, and I knew he was having the same hunger pains. I backed away slowly, glancing at Ajax who looked uneasy. I didn't like it when he was uneasy.

"What?"

"Pool. Do you play?" Wes asked, wincing.

I shook my head.

"I did." He bit his bottom lip and doubled over briefly. "Wasn't bad either. Could make a hundred bucks in friendly games on a good night."

I doubled over this time. "This isn't a good idea." I placed my hands on my knees and sucked in some air. Standing up straight, I saw another figure in the shadows. It was a woman I did not recognize. She was heavy-set, dirty-blonde hair, wearing a smock. She was dressed like the woman who used to do my mom's hair.

Wes saw that I had noticed the woman. "My sister," he said. "The real Lou..." He stopped himself. "Not real, exactly, A Throwaway version of my sister Lou. Say hello, Lou."

"Hello, Lou," the woman said.

Wes slapped the table and let out a snort of laughter. "That is just like something she would say, too. I swear these Throwaways ain't too bad once you get used to them." He saw Throwaway June and pointed at her. "You got April's?" He snuck a step to his left. He didn't think I noticed, but I did. He was going to make his move.

I nodded. "April's not feeling like herself, so I invited Throwaway June to tag along." I stepped back again.

Drool formed at the corner of Wes's mouth. "There's a lot of that going around. Not feeling like yourself."

"Yeah," I said, "there is."

He licked his bottom lip and laughed. "I ain't exactly hidin' my intentions, am I?"

Ajax let out a low rumbling growl.

"Not really, no. You forget. I'm in the same boat you're in."

He laughed, "But you ain't no fat man. I tried to eat a Twinkie yesterday, and threw it right up. A Twinkie, Oz. I love those damn things."

"Where'd you get a Twinkie?"

He smiled and put his hand over his mouth. "Oops. I let the cat out of the bag. Half my backpack is Twinkies. I stock up wherever we go and keep them all to myself."

I must have looked shocked and hurt because he immediately started to defend himself.

"You just don't know, Oz. I gotta have my Twinkies. Nothing I like more. 'Cept maybe slicing you up and eating you up in a soup. Man, I have just been craving soup. Human soup."

That did sound good. It was my turn to drool. I lifted my hand to wipe the spittle from the corners of my mouth. I must have shifted my gaze enough in doing so for Wes to take the opportunity to rush me. He charged me like a bull. I didn't have time to react. His big meaty hand grabbed my shirt collar and yanked me towards him. The look on his face was the same I had seen on the old man when he was plotting to eat his prey. It was a sickening look of anticipation and joy.

"Nothing personal, Oz, but a fat man has got to eat."

His intention was to pick me up and slam me down on the pool table, but he was on his back on the floor before he could carry out his plan. Ajax's fang-filled mouth was just inches from his face.

"Get off me! I gotta eat!" He squirmed under Ajax's tremendous weight.

I looked down and happened to see his lower calf exposed. I pictured myself dropping down and quickly tearing the flesh from the bone. Just one bite. That would be enough. That might get me through the day. I considered the best way to approach it over and over again. Just bite, rip, tear, and eat. Bite, rip, tear, and eat. That's all it would take. I closed my eyes trying to shake the thought. I couldn't go through with it, could I? I could. Yes, I could. Nobody would blame me. The Flish was in me. I had an excuse. I felt myself smile, and I saw the Flish doing the same thing in my mind's eye... I wasn't about to let him win.

I stepped through the doorway and ran to another door down the short hall. It was locked, but it only slowed me down. My adrenaline was high. Two solid kicks near the door knob and the door popped open. I rushed through and found myself standing in the banquet hall. I took a few seconds to collect myself and let Throwaway June catch up. I yelled back at Ajax to keep holding Wes down.

"C'mon," I said to Throwaway June, noticing a slight change in her hair color and maybe the length, too. I couldn't be sure, but I figured it didn't really matter all that much.

"It's safe, Ajax!" I said once we reached the other end of the banquet hall.

A few minutes later the big gorilla was standing on all fours next to me. "Thanks," I said.

He grinned.

I patted him on the back. "I think it's time we talked about what to do if we don't... you know, make it out of here."

His nostrils flared, and he looked away.

"It's important," I said. "Archie and Bobby are upstairs. We gotta make sure they make it out of here. They lost their Keeper, so we need to have a backup plan..."

Ajax knuckle-walked away. I thought about making him listen, but in the end, I knew he'd do the right thing. He didn't need me to tell him what he had to do. I was about to follow him when I heard my name from the other end of the huge room. Wes stood in the doorway, and I could see that he was crying.

"I'm sorry, boy. I'm so, so sorry."

I choked back a tear.

"I can't hold out much longer, Oz."

I nodded. "None of us can."

"Lock me up. Chain me down. You gotta do something."

"Can't. Not unless I do the same to everybody, including me. Otherwise you'll be defenseless when one of us finds you, and trust me, one of us will."

He shook his head. "I don't care, boy. I used up my last drop of willpower. If I do anything to any of you... I just can't live with myself. I'd rather it be me."

"Wes!" I barked. "Gordy, April, even Tyrone, I can do without them. But when it comes time for me to stand and fight, I need you and I need Lou. I can count on you two. I don't care if I do look like a big juicy steak to you right now, I know you'll come through for me when I need you."

He roared and smashed his fist into the wall.

I left before I actually gave in to his pleas.

"You're making a mistake, boy!" were his parting words.

And I thought he was probably right. But what I didn't tell him was the minute I had heard him ask to be chained down, I was coming up with a plan to take advantage of the situation, and eat him myself.

***

I sent Ajax to get Lou. I no longer trusted the radio. Giving away my position did nothing but let the others know where they could find a meal. Actually, Tyrone and Wes were the only ones I had to worry about. April was locked in the closet, and Gordy wasn't going anywhere in the condition he was in. But Tyrone alone was enough to concern me. It seemed like he wanted to hurt me and everyone else for that matter even before the infection.

I sat on the floor near the front entrance. Every sound the old house made sent me into a defensive posture. I was sure Tyrone was coming for me. But, they all proved to be nothing. When Lou finally arrived, I was just one big frazzled nerve.

I didn't even say hello. I just started interrogating her. "What did you find out from Bobby?"

She looked a little offended that I didn't seem happy to see her. I was. Had I been myself I would have told her how much I missed her, more than she could possibly know. But I was way past being myself.

"As far as I can tell, there's some kind of king involved."

"What, like the king of England or something?"

"Not sure what he's king of, but he's either the Keeper or Creyshaw for this story."

"You don't know for sure? What have you been doing?" I sounded a lot harsher than I'd intended.

"Getting straight answers from Bobby isn't exactly the easiest thing in the world, you know? Besides, it doesn't do you any good to know who this king is because the Flish is already here. He... ate the Creyshaw, remember? It's too late. Keeper or Creyshaw, king does you no good."

"He hasn't made it all the way through," I said. "Don't you see? He's stuck in this house. Maybe the Creyshaw failed, but that only got him this far. It's got something to do with that stupid package..."

"Package?" Lou snapped her fingers. "That's right."

"What?"

"I asked him about the package and the only answer he would give is some little poem... I thought it was just a bunch of mumbo-jumbo."

"Nothing is just mumbo-jumbo in this world. What was the poem?"

She titled her head up and to the right as she tried to remember. I saw her silently mouth a few words. "From," she started. "From here to the next. From alive...no, wait. From dead to alive. He cannot find... detect. He cannot detect. For the package to arrive."

"From here to the next," I said. "From dead to alive. He cannot detect for the package to arrive."

"That's it," she said. "It doesn't make sense."

I repeated the poem to myself and then out loud a few more times. I got to the word detect. I didn't know why, but it made me stop. "Detect. Detect. Detect. There's something about that word."

"Well," Lou said, "it means to find or discover something, so it means we have to find the package."

"Maybe," I said, barely able to pay attention because I was so focused on that one word. Detect... It hit me. "Detective."

Lou nodded. "Yeah, they detect. It's actually in the word."

"No, you said a king, but that's not it. It's the king. Detective King."

"Who's Detective King?"

"He's the cop, back in the Land of the Dead. He's the one looking for Fish, only he doesn't know he's looking for Fish. He cannot detect for the package to arrive. Detective King can't find the package in order for Fish to arrive."

"But Fish is here?"

"No, he's here and he's there. Fish can't escape the Land of the Dead until he finds his package. He's nothing without his package. He won't leave it."

"How do you know?"

"You should see him when he doesn't have that package. He goes nuts without it."

Lou shook her head. "It doesn't fit the rules of the other Storytellers. A Destroyer can come forward when a Storyteller is captured, right?"

"That's the way Ajax explained it, but Tarek said there is a way to bind the Flish to the Keeper, to keep him from spreading his infection."

"What else did he say?

I didn't tell her that he said there was basically no hope, that I should kill her and the others and live my life craving human flesh, so I just told her that he was his regular chatty self and added that he wasn't a lot of help.

"How do we bind the Flish to the Keeper?"

I shrugged. "He didn't know."

She startled me by snapping her fingers. "It's King. He's got to be the Keeper."

I thought it over. "Maybe."

She tapped her finger on her lips. "And the package... maybe we have to get it to King. That's how we bind Fish to him, right?"

"We'll have to figure that out as we go. We've got to pick a strategy and go with it. This is the closest thing to a theory we've had since we've been here. I've got to go back to the Land of the Dead and find Detective King..." I stopped when I realized that just finding him wasn't enough. How was I going to talk to him? As far as I could tell, Fish was the only one who saw me in the Land of the Dead.

"Finding King's only part of it. What about the package? How do you get that to him?"

We had a lot to figure out with only four days left. "Bobby's got to know more," I said.

"I'll try," she said, but the look on her face said it all. Bobby had given her all the information he had. "What do we do in the meantime?"

"I need to find out more about Fish."

"Okay, how?"

"An old friend," I said.

***

Wes sat at one end of the dining table in the banquet hall, and I sat at the other. It was just enough distance to keep us from smelling each other. I hoped it would keep us from trying to tear each other apart.

Lou marveled at Wes's Throwaway sister Lou. She had heard stories about the woman for years, and meeting her or a version of her was weird for Lou.

"I thought you said I looked like her," Lou said.

Wes smiled. "When she was a youngster. This is her three kids later. She... puffed up a bit after that. But that's how she is in my mind, I guess."

"Ask him," I shouted from the other end of the table.

Lou lingered on Throwaway Lou's face just a second longer and then gave her undivided attention to Wes. "We need to know everything you know about Fish."

"Fish? The kind with gills and fins?"

"No," I moaned. "Albert Fish!"

He laughed. "Oh. That makes sense. Well, let's see... you're asking me to go way back. My uncle was a bit of nut. Into serial killers, believed in Bigfoot, thought Elvis was still alive. Off his rocker, really, but he was fun to be around."

I cleared my throat as loudly as I could.

"I think he's trying to tell you to speed it up," Lou said.

"This is part of my remembering process. I gotta set the mood. Albert Fish, died in the electric chair in... 1936. Convicted of killing six kids, I believe, but claimed there were hundreds. He usually abducted children society tried to hide anyway so he didn't get caught for years."

"Sick," Lou said.

"Yeah, he wasn't exactly the kind of guy you'd ask to babysit your kids. My uncle thought he was the worst serial killer of them all because he was so meek and mild. He looked like someone's grandfather. They trusted him. The weird part is that Fish claimed that he was the son of God and by eating the kids he was making sure they made it to heaven."

"His tools," I said. Knowing that I would have to shout to communicate with Wes, Lou and I had discussed the questions ahead of time so she could do it for me. The trouble was, she was just letting him babble on about unimportant stuff.

"Do you know anything about his tools?"

"His tools?"

"He always has them with him in the Land of the Dead," she said. "We thinks it's a way to beat him."

"You do, do you?" Wes asked looking at me. "Well, they were called his tools of terror. He butchered children with them. What else do you need to know?"

"Do you know what happened to them?" Lou asked.

"Goodness, no," Wes said. "Wouldn't want to know a thing like that."

"They're in this house," I yelled.

"You know that for sure?" Wes asked.

I hesitated. "Pretty sure."

"Got any idea where?"

"The old man is tied to the basement. He can't leave there for very long. Oz and I think they're down there."

"That's a big basement. How we going to find them?"

"Well," Lou said, "Oz thought we could look in shifts. First I gotta move Gordy out of there. He's in no shape to help with the search. You take the basement during the night. Start in the bowling alley and search every inch of it. I'll help. Oz will come in during the day and pick up where you left off. I'll help him, too."

"When you going to sleep?"

"I'll sleep when this over."

"What about Tyrone?" Wes asked. "He should help."

"No," I barked from the other end of the table. "We need to leave him out of this."

"Why?" Wes asked.

I saw Lou put her hand on top of his. "We just think it would be for the best."

"Okay," he said. "One question. What do we do with the tools if we find them?"

Lou looked down at me for an answer, but I didn't offer one. She turned to Wes. "We're still trying to figure that one out."

***

The dead boy came for Throwaway June and me late in the evening. I pleaded with him for help. I told him that I thought I knew what I needed to do, but I wanted some answers from him. I wanted to get the package to King, but I didn't know how. I insisted that he tell me, but he was his usual silent self. He wasn't offering any help at all. All he did was walk us through another portal to the Land of the Dead.

It was a bright afternoon. We were in the country somewhere. All that there was before us was a dirt road surrounded by woods on either side.

Throwaway June, whose hair was clearly darker and shorter now, grabbed my hand. She obviously didn't like the place. As pleasant as the weather was, there was an overriding feeling that we could discover something horrible and disturbing at any moment.

We rounded a bend. Tucked away behind a row of plush green trees was a small, two-story house. The paint was faded, and the roof needed patching.

The dead boy approached and stopped at the edge of the property. Throwaway June and I stood beside him not wanting to get any closer to the house. In the most subtle way, he suggested that we needed to go on without him. He rarely looked you in the eyes, but when he did, it meant a lot. He peered up at me and conveyed his meaning very clearly to me. "Go on without me."

I stepped on the bent grass with Throwaway June still holding my hand. We were half way to the house when we heard what sounded like humming. Turning to our left, we saw Grace picking flowers where the woods met the yard. The old man was nowhere to be seen.

I dragged June over to her and did something that I knew was pointless. I talked to her.

"Grace, you have to find a way to hear me. You're in danger. You can't be here."

She gave no indication that she could hear me.

"Please, Grace, listen. There's got to be a way you can hear me. This man, Mr. Howard, he's a bad man. He's a scary man."

Still nothing from her.

"Grace."

I heard a noise from the house and turned quickly on my heels. Throw-way June gripped my hand tightly. I pried her fingers from mine and told her to wait with Grace.

I was tired of this. I could end this. Why else would I be in the Land of the Dead? I was there to stop him, and nothing was going to prevent me from doing just that.

I bolted through the door and found the old gray man organizing pots and pans on the kitchen counter. The clanging of metal and iron was almost deafening. He held a frying pan in his hand and seemed to marvel at the weight and size of it.

"Can't beat an iron skillet for frying up the fatty meats. The trick is to leave it thick enough to sink your teeth into, but not so thick it leaves the center uncooked. Got to be able to fry it up quick."

I approached.

"I tell you what. The meat I get from these young'uns is better than your fanciest store bought."

Close enough to take a swing, I tightened my fists, swung away and passed right through him.

He laughed. "Good thing you couldn't hit me because you wouldn't do nothing but tick me off. As you can guess, I'm not a good person to tick off."

"Neither am I," I said.

He laughed again. "You're harmless. Here anyway."

"I could say the same about you. You should see how pathetic you are in my world."

"I imagine it's a lot like you are here."

I grimaced. I would give anything to pound his brains in.

"There's really no reason we can't be friends. If you would just take a minute to think about this, I'm not the bad guy here.

I'm offering these children a chance to go to heaven through me."

"You're sick."

"That's what they always say about men who see things as clearly as I do. We all have a purpose, Oz."

I raised an eyebrow. He'd used my name, and I didn't like it.

"My purpose is to save the children from an impure life. Their purpose is to make their families realize that they didn't love enough. They won't make the same mistake again. All because of me."

"You can't believe all this crap you're spewing."

"As much as you believe you can undo what you did to Stevie Dayton and bring back the world."

"How do you know..."

"The end is the end, Oz. You can't change that."

I had heard enough. I turned to leave. On my way to the door, I saw his package sitting on a well-worn coffee table in the living room. I peered over my shoulder to see if he was watching. Fortunately, he was busy preparing the rest of his ingredients for the stew he planned on eating later that night.

I walked over to the coffee table and whispered, "Please, let me do this." I reached down and my hand went through the package and past the coffee table. I grabbed for it a couple more times thinking it was just a matter of concentration. But, each time, my hand passed through the package as if it were nothing more than air. I reached way back and brought my hand forward with as much speed as I could build, thinking now that it was a matter of grabbing it before it had a chance to become formless. My hand passed through, and I stumbled to the left losing my balance in the attempt. I stumbled and fell to the floor with a bang.

I closed my eyes for just a second to get my bearings. When I reopened them, I was in the Winter Gardens. My trip to the

Land of the Dead was over before it started. I shook my head in disgust. I had failed to figure out a way to get the package. It was hopeless. There was no way I could bring it out of the Land of the Dead, and I wasn't real confident we were going find it in time inside the huge mansion.

I sat up and pulled my knees to my chest, wrapping my arms around my shins. We were done. I glanced up and noticed Throwaway June (who actually wasn't June at all anymore . . . her hair was darker and she seemed much smaller) holding a wildflower in her hand. All the plants in the garden were long since dead, so it didn't seem likely that she had gotten it from there.

"Where did you get that?"

The Throwaway's eyebrows came together in the middle of her forehead and she looked puzzled. "Have I done something wrong?"

"No, I just want to know where you got the flower."

"She gave it to me."

"She? Grace?"

She nodded.

I felt a smile form on my face.

DAY 7

EIGHTEEN

"We have a way," I said grabbing Lou by the shoulders. I was so excited I had the urge to pull her close and plant a kiss on her lips. I could barely contain myself.

A smile crept across her face. "We can get the package?"

"And get it to King."

"How?"

"It's the Throwaways. They can communicate with the people in the Land of the Dead, and June brought a flower back with her." I held it up and showed it to Lou.

She took it from me. "We have a way."

"Now all I have to do is bring a Throwaway with me to the Land of the Dead, find Fish, distract him, and the Throwaway can grab the package."

"And King, how do we get it to him?"

"Easy. We find him in the Land of the Dead the next day. The Throwaway just hands it to him."

Her eyes moved back and forth as she seemed to be playing out the scenario in her head.

"What's wrong?"

"It just sounds too simple."

"It will work," I insisted. "I know it."

She wanted to believe it as much as I did, so she nodded and allowed an impossible grin to light up her face. It was a beautiful sight. I couldn't get over how safe and perfect everything felt just being with her, even in this insane version of the world. Lou made everything make sense to me.

"Why you looking at me all goofy?" she asked.

I was shocked by her question. I let go of her and backed away. "What? Can't a guy be happy?"

"Yeah, but you looked like... you were going to kiss me or something?"

I furrowed my brow and narrowed my gaze. "Kiss you? C'mon, you're Lou."

"Meaning?"

"I don't know. I've known you since... well, a long time now. You were a dirty little rug rat when I first met you."

"And you were a pinhead jerk. Not much has changed."

"Don't get mad because I don't want to kiss you."

She chuckled. "Relieved is more like it."

"Good. Then it's settled. Neither one of us wants to kiss the other one."

She nodded emphatically and crossed her arms.

"Maybe I've thought about it," I said for reasons that are unclear to me. The words just fell out of my mouth.

"You have?" She looked intrigued in spite of herself.

"Sure. You're pretty."

She blushed.

"And I like things about you."

"Like what?"

I rolled my eyes. "I don't think we have time for this."

"We've got time," she said.

"Well, you smell nice."

"I smell nice?"

"You don't stink, I mean. Even when you do. You always smell like Lou."

"Okay," she said. "I guess that's a compliment."

"Your eyes are nice. I like those."

She rolled her eyes this time. "You're terrible at this."

"At what?"

"Telling someone what you like about them."

I grunted and stepped toward her. "If you really have to know, there's not much I don't like about you. I think about you and I smile. I could be in an all out brawl for my life against the meanest monster in this crazy world and the smallest thought of you comes to me and I smile. No matter what happens to me, I think that at least I got a chance to know Lou and spend time with her and, yes, even dream about kissing her."

Her eyes smiled. "You dream about kissing me?"

"Every chance I get."

I can't recall where the distance between us went. I don't know how my hands found their way to her face. I don't know why my head moved forward, but it did, slowly, and I was pulling her closer to me. The split-second I felt her soft lips touch mine, my heart slammed against my chest. I knew instantly that she really was my one true love. The longer the kiss lasted the lighter my heart felt. It may be terrible to say, but at that moment, I didn't care if we ever made it back home. I was where I belonged.

***

That was my first kiss, my first love, the first time in a long time that I didn't wonder about what horrible thing was going to happen next. Where I was didn't matter. Getting home didn't matter. Figuring out the crazy world I was trapped in didn't matter.

I sat in the banquet room with Ajax at my side. I was so giddy it was hard to focus on what I needed to do. I had to go the Land of the Dead. I had to take June with me, even though she was clearly no longer presenting herself as June. Her face had completely changed. It was paler and smoother. And her hair was black and shorter now. Some of the elements of June's face were there, but they were quickly fading.

Her appearance didn't matter. She could be turning into Abraham Lincoln for all I cared. Her ability to interact with the ghosts in the Land of the Dead and bring objects back was what mattered.

I turned to give Ajax some last minute instructions, but he was gone. The banquet hall was gone. The house was gone. I was standing in the middle of the road with June next to me. It was late in the game, but I was realizing that no two trips to The Land of the Dead were exactly the same.

A cool breeze rustled the brown leaves clinging to the almost bare trees, and disrupted the piles of leaves on the side of the road. I scanned up and down the street. I knew this place. I couldn't recall from where, but I definitely knew this place.

The houses and cars in the driveway did tell me one thing for sure. I was not in the right time period. This was not Albert Fish's time.

"Hey!" I yelled. The dead boy was not around. We were wasting time by being here. I needed to be back in the Fish's time so we could get his tools of terror. "Where are you?"

There was no answer. I looked up and down the street and then just started walking. The direction didn't matter because I didn't know where I was anyway. I just walked in the direction I was facing.

We reached a side street, and I nearly gasped at the name on the street sign, Westwood Drive. My house was on Westwood Drive. I peered through the trees at the house immediately to my left. It was Donnie Kaye's house. A kid three years ahead of me in school. I was in Tullahoma!

I felt a mixture of joy and total annoyance at finding myself in my old hometown. It was good to be in familiar surroundings, and if I wasn't on such a strict timetable I would be running towards my house at that very moment, but I didn't need to be here, not now. I needed to be where Fish was.

"Where are you?" I asked the empty street again. I felt a tugging on my arm and looked down to discover it was June. She pointed straight ahead. I looked where she was pointing, but didn't see what she was seeing. "What is it?"

"Stevie," she said.

I bent my head forward and tried to sharpen my focus by squinting my yes. Finally, I saw someone move through the trees thirty feet or so ahead. He was wearing a yellow jacket and black mittens.

"Stevie," I called out.

Upon hearing his name, I could see him tense up. I stepped forward and he took off down the street.

"Stevie, wait! How did you get here?" I chased after him with June not far behind me. "I thought I told you to stay with Gordy."

"Gordy's mean," he yelled without turning.

"I know he can be a jerk, but..."

He cut through a yard and dashed through a thin strip of trees behind the house. I couldn't believe it, but I think I knew where he was going. He was going to Stevie's real house. How would a Throwaway know this shortcut to Stevie's house? I guess he could have plucked it from Gordy's memory banks, but it seemed totally remarkable to me.

Since I knew where he was going, it didn't seem necessary to follow him at full speed. I was getting winded, and there was at least a quarter of a mile to go. I slowed to a jog, and tried to clear my head. I wasn't in the time period I needed to be in, so the question was, why was I here and where was the dead boy? It seemed strange to change things up on me now, just when I was so close to bringing down the Flish.

We exited the woods and turned up the street towards Stevie's house. Visiting Stevie's house was never high on my list of things to do, but it seemed like I was always brought back here for some reason or another.

I cast my head down and concentrated on my footfalls. When I reached a familiar crack in the street, I knew that when I looked up I'd see Stevie's house just a block away. I counted to three and lifted my head.

As much as I hoped it wouldn't be, it was there. I caught the storm door rattling to a close.

June looked up at me and smiled. She had no idea what that house meant to me, and it shouldn't have bothered me, but I wanted to knock that stupid smile of her face. To my horror, she kept the smile until we were standing at the front door of the house.

"Stevie," I said.

I heard a door slam, so I quickly stepped through the foyer and stood at the head of the hallway. Every door was open except the door at the very end of the hall. I immediately began to sweat. "The basement," I whispered.

"Stevie," I said "we shouldn't be here."

A bang came from basement.

I dropped my head and said. "CRAP! I am so tired of having to creep through dark basements. I'd like for once to have to go into a well-lit, completely un-scary room."

I slinked down the hall with June tagging along. Reaching the basement, I placed my hand on the door knob and said, "Come on, Stevie. Please don't make me come down there. Just come upstairs and we'll get out of here."

No answer.

I turned the knob and pushed the door open. The stairs looked like jagged teeth to me. I stepped down on the first one and imagined myself stepping into a monster's mouth and walking down its throat. The feeling stuck with me until I stood on the basement floor.

"Where are we?" June asked.

"The belly," I said.

"What?"

"Nothing," I said. The sound of something scraping across the dirty concrete floor came from our left. Once our eyes adjusted to the dim light, I could see Stevie sitting in a chair and kicking the dirt.

"I'm sorry, Oz," he said.

"That's all right," I answered. "Let's just go."

"I didn't want to make all those bad things happen."

"What bad things?"

"He said it would make us smarter and everybody would like us."

My mouth went dry. My legs felt like wet noodles, and I heard a buzzing in my ears. This wasn't Throwaway Stevie. It was the real Stevie.

"You don't have to be sorry, Stevie."

"But I did bad things."

"It's not your fault." I looked above him and saw the pipe that he had tied the rope to when he ended his life. His death was what brought the first Destroyer into our world.

"Dr. Bashir said the bad people must pay. None of us wanted to do it."

"I know, Stevie. We shouldn't have been bad people." I was standing in front of him now. I knelt down. "If I could do it all over again, Stevie, I promise you I would be nicer. I wouldn't treat you the way I did. It's not your fault I'm here. It's my fault. I deserve to be here."

He whispered, "But not for the reason you think."

"What do you mean?"

"You're here because I see the magic in you."

I smiled and sarcastically said, "Where have I heard that before?"

He looked puzzled. "You heard it from Lou. Do you like her?"

I nodded. "I do."

He smiled. "I knew you would."

I patted his leg. "You've got good taste, buddy."

"Mom said I had a knack for drawing pretty girls."

I looked over my shoulder and looked at June. Seeing her fading face jarred my memory. "Listen, Stevie, I'd love to sit down here with you and chat, but I gotta find..."

"The Flish," he said. "He made Connie really sad. Dr. Bashir said he had to be in her story. Said he had done bad, bad things to people like us. Tried to do something bad to his great uncle a long, long time ago. Before Dr. Bashir was even alive. 'Put him in your story,' he said. 'He'll make the other bad people pay. Bad against bad.'"

"Bad against bad," I repeated and leaned in closer. "How do I get everyone home, Stevie?"

"I once read the story backwards," he said.

I laughed. "That's great, Stevie, but I need to know how I can end this. How do I get everyone home?"

"When you read it backwards, it's not the same. It changes."

"Stevie, concentrate. How do I get everyone home? You like Lou, right? You want her to find her way home, don't you?"

He titled his head and was clearly considering my question. "She doesn't have a home."

I turned that over in my head. "I don't understand. What do

you mean she doesn't have a home?"

He shrugged. "I don't know. I guess I mean she doesn't have a house with people in it."

"What are you saying?"

"I'm saying words," he said.

I was getting frustrated. "Yes, but the words you're saying aren't making any sense. Lou has to have a home. She came from somewhere. Everybody does."

He pointed at June. "She doesn't."

"Yes, but she's a Throwaway..."

"A never-was," Stevie said.

I stood up. "What are you saying?"

"I told you, I'm saying words."

I didn't like the words he was saying. If he was telling me that Lou was a never-was, not real, I didn't want to hear it. It couldn't be true. She was real. She had to be.

"You look sad," Stevie said.

I didn't say anything.

The ground began to shake.

"They're coming back," Stevie said.

"Who?"

The basement floor began to crack. June screamed and ran up the stairs.

"June, stop!" I turned to chase her, but Stevie grabbed my arm.

As if he was trying to force his words into my skull, he spoke slowly and harshly. "It's never the same if you read it backwards. You see things you didn't see before."

He let go of my arm and stumbled backwards, tripping over the debris from the crumbling basement floor. I struggled to keep on my feet, but I crashed down on my elbow and felt a burning, numbing sensation throughout my arm. I gritted my teeth and sucked in a long stream of air. By the time I had worked through the pain and stood up, Stevie was gone. The house continued to shake, and the crack in the floor grew wider.

I made it to the bottom step of the basement stairs when a gigantic, gnarled, clawed hand burst through the concrete. Now I knew who was coming back. Takers. I ran, barely touching the surface of the stairs with my feet. I was in the hallway before my mind caught up. "June!"

A shadow moved to my right. A door was open to one of the rooms. Behind me I heard the tell-tale chatter of the Taker coming from the basement. I quickly approached the open door. June stood in front me, shaking and facing the wall above the dresser.

I entered. "C'mon, June. We've got to go."

She raised her arm and pointed at the wall.

I followed with my eyes. There, hanging on the wall, just as it was the last time I saw it, was the perfectly drawn, framed picture of a Délon. Their source. What they were so desperately looking for. I ran to it and attempted to rip it from the wall, but my hand passed through. I tried again. I tried a third time before it hit me. I was in the Land of the Dead.

"June, you have to grab it."

She hesitated. I heard the Taker coming up the stairs.

"Hurry," I barked.

She didn't hurry. It seemed like she was walking as slowly as she possibly could.

"June, we've got to get out of here. I need that picture. Please, hurry."

The Taker roared. He was at the top of the stairs.

Still June took her time.

I rushed to the door and carefully peeked down the hallway. It was there. It was almost too broad for the hall. It ducked its head so as not to hit the ceiling. Its eyes zeroed in on me. Crouching, it opened its mouth and let out a high-pitched wail. I grabbed the door and hurried to push it shut, but in the blink of an eye the ugly beast was standing in the doorway. I put all my weight into the door and managed to shut it. I turned to see June holding the framed picture of the Délon in her hand.

"Out the window," I said, fighting hyperventilation.

The Taker pushed on the door, and I comically tried to prevent the monster from opening it. It was like a bug trying to push back the moon. I heard what sounded like a crack of thunder and then felt myself tumbling through the air. A tremendous white light washed out the room.

My head slapped against a hard wooden surface. I heard a roar and looked up bleary-eyed. I felt instantly relieved to see Ajax staring back at me.

DAY 8

NINETEEN

There was no ice, so Lou rubbed the back of my neck trying to work out the throbbing pain in my head. The trip coming back from the Land of the Dead this time around was definitely much worse than the trip there.

"So the trip was a total waste of time?" Lou asked.

I went over the conversation I'd had with Stevie in my head. It was a little hazy due to the crack I took to the skull but, unfortunately, I could recall the gist of it. Lou was a never-was.

"Not totally," I said. "June brought back something." I looked around the table and didn't see June. Pulling away from Lou, I stood up and a wave of panic hit me. "June... where's June?"

"Right there," she pointed to a little girl with black hair.

I couldn't make out her face so I approached her and wasn't totally surprised to discover she looked remarkably like Grace.

"What did she bring back?" Lou asked.

I examined June's face for a beat longer and then asked her, "Do you have it?"

She nodded, reached down, and picked up the framed picture.

I took it from her and showed it to Lou. "We've got what the Délons have been looking for."

"The source," she said just before a smile spread across her face. "We have it. We own them."

"Don't get ahead of yourself," I said. "We don't know how it works."

"But we know they desperately want it. They've lost control of this world without it. They don't even know what the source is. This is huge."

"True," I said. "But that doesn't really help us. Besides we've only got today and tomorrow left on our nine days. Having this will mean nothing if we can't get the Flish's package to Detective King..."

"Where is she?" Wes screamed from the other end of the room.

"Who?" I screamed back.

"You know who! What have you done with Lou, my Lou?"

"The Throwaway?" I asked.

"Is that all she was to you? Someone who doesn't matter? She wasn't just a Throwaway! She was my sister! What did you do with her?"

"Wes," Lou said, "Oz didn't do anything to your sister."

"Don't cover for him, Lou. He's the reason we're here in the first place."

"You're not making any sense," I said. "Why would I do anything to your Throwaway?"

"Stop calling her that!" He stomped towards us.

The closer he got, the stronger his smell became. It was like bacon sizzling in a frying pan. Mouthwatering. I hadn't eaten in... too long.

"Don't come any closer," I begged.

Either he didn't hear me or he just didn't car; he continued coming at us.

"Wes," Lou said.

Ajax plodded towards him.

"Out of the way, go-rilla," Wes said.

"Wes, you don't know what you're doing!" Lou shouted

I headed for the door and stopped in my tracks when I saw Tyrone staring back at me from the hallway. My stomach twisted. I doubled over from the pain.

"They're all gone," Tyrone said.

Wes stopped at the sound of his voice.

I positioned myself behind Lou.

"Gone where?" Lou asked.

"The old man," Tyrone answered. "Got Valerie last night. Gordy's Throwaway is gone, too." He stepped into the room and moved around the table. He held tight to his hunting knife. "Yours is the only one left, far as I can tell."

Wes wiped the drool from his mouth with the back of his hand. "Got 'em all but the golden boy's. Why you suppose that is?" He was clearly sizing the situation up, trying to determine if he was closer to me or Tyrone. I knew that's what he was thinking because I was thinking the same thing.

"We can't be in the same room," I said in a voice I didn't even recognize. It was low and weak. The hunger was more than I could take.

"We've got a plan," Lou said. "You just have to hold out a little bit longer."

"Can't hold out," Wes said. His head was down, but his eyes were looking straight at us. "I've got to eat!"

"We all do," I snapped. "But we can't."

"Can't ain't an option," Tyrone said. "We eat or we die."

A hideous laughter came from the walls, a hardy cackling. The old man's voice surrounded us. "And they shall eat every one the flesh of his friend in the siege."

I stepped out from behind Lou. "Can't is an option, Tyrone. He's not going to win. This is..." I counted the days in my head. "This is the beginning of day eight. Give me until the end of day nine and this will be over. I promise you."

"That ain't a promise you can keep," Wes said.

"Shut up," Lou screamed. "We are family. Family believes in each other. Family is there for each other. I'm through with this whole thing. The old man cannot turn us against each other. Wes, back in your little room. Tyrone, second floor, now."

They looked at Lou perplexed and then started to laugh.

"Upstairs, huh?" Tyrone smiled. He shrugged his shoulders and started to back out of the room, stopping at the doorway. "Just between us, I was getting used to having that Throwaway around. Took my mind off the hunger. It was nice having... her around again."

"It wasn't her," I said.

"The real Valerie will always be with you, Tyrone," Lou said placing her hand over her heart.

He nodded and disappeared into the hallway.

Wes had started his retreat back to his room. He stopped when he reached the end of the table and turned back to us. "Boy, I don't feel like much of a man no more. Seems like I'm always letting kids fight my battles for me, and I ain't doing much in return. You get us out of this one, and I promise you the next one is mine."

Lou was about to say something, but I grabbed her arm. She was going to tell him that was all right. That he'd done enough. That he was an important part of our group. We wouldn't be anywhere without him. All that was true, but he wouldn't have believed any of it, not at that moment.

"Sure thing, Wes," I said. "Next one's yours."

***

Lou, Throwaway Grace (formerly June), and I stood in the deep end of the empty pool. Ajax sat at the top of the ladder keeping a watchful eye over us.

I was panicked. We couldn't waste another trip to the Land of the Dead. I wanted to talk to the dead boy, but I didn't know how to get in contact with him, so I just talked to the thin air.

"Listen. You have to take us to the old man, in his time. We can't afford to go anywhere else. I don't know how this works, but please, take us to Fish." I stepped forward and felt a faint coldness on my feet. The thought went in and out of my mind. I had more important things to worry about than my feet being cold. "Hey, little... dead... boy."

"Little dead boy?" Lou asked with a tone that suggested she was disgusted with me. "You don't know his name?"

"He doesn't talk much. I never got his name. And I'm not so sure if you should be talking, by the way. He might not come if he knows you're here. Your job is to make sure the old man doesn't get June-Grace or whatever her name is while she and I wait for our ride to the Land of the Dead." My ankles were cold now. "Is it getting cold in here?"

"Water," Lou said.

"What?" I said turning to her. I was surprised to see her standing in ten inches of water. I looked down at my feet and was even more surprised to see that I was standing in water, too. "What the..." is all I managed to say before we were instantaneously immersed in water. There wasn't even time to hold our breath. I wanted to cough but couldn't. Lou, Grace, and I scrambled up towards the top. I'm not even sure why. We had no way of knowing if there was a top. But still we kicked and pushed our way up.

I got a glimpse of a figure floating a few feet away. The dead boy. It had to be. I peered through the darkness and saw his face. My cousin Anthony. I changed direction and swam towards him. Inches away, I reached out, grabbed his hand, and fought to find the surface of the water. Seconds passed and I finally broke through. I inhaled as much air as I could, coughing violently as I released it. Lou and Grace had also made it to the surface. They were gasping for air. I zipped around to look at my cousin Anthony only to find it wasn't him at all. It was the dead boy.

"What happened? Where are we?" I heard Lou ask.

I looked around. "The pool, it filled up with water."

She sloshed around in the water looking in every direction. "Where's Ajax? And why are the lights suddenly working?"

"The Land of the Dead," I said.

"What?"

"We're in the pool in the Land of the Dead." I turned to the dead boy. "This is when Fish worked here, isn't it?"

He did what he always did. He didn't answer.

"I don't understand," Lou said. "What am I doing here?"

***

We stood on the side of the pool dripping wet. I had almost forgotten why I hated the water so much, but finding myself underwater for however brief a time it was, reminded me of the horrible sensation of drowning that I had lived through when I was a kid. Now I was convinced that hate wasn't a strong enough word for how I felt about the water.

"I died when I was a baby," Lou said.

"What?"

"That has to be it. I died when I was a baby for like a minute or something and the doctors brought me back. That's how I was able to cross over to the Land of the Dead. I died when I was a baby. My parents just never told me."

"Must be it," I said. I didn't want to tell her what Stevie had told me. She wasn't what he said she was. She was real. As real as me and Wes and the others. She had to be. She was right. She died when she was a baby. Her parents just never told her because that's not the kind of thing you tell someone. Why would you? Stevie was wrong.

"Well, I'm here, whatever the reason. What's the plan?"

"If I'm right, this is the time Fish worked as a painter for the mansion. We need to find the old man."

"How?" Lou asked.

The dead boy started to walk away.

"We follow him," I said.

He took us through a maze of hallways and rooms. The house was alive with activity. We didn't see anyone, but we heard what sounded like an army of people working just ahead of us.

"What do we tell people we're doing here?" Lou asked.

"They can't see us," I said. "We're like ghosts."

"We're the ghosts?"

I laughed. "I know. It sounds weird..."

"Can I help you?" a woman's voice called out from behind us.

I stiffened. It was impossible. She couldn't be talking to us. Grace. Of course. She could see Grace.

We slowly turned and saw a woman dressed in a floor-length black dress and a white bonnet. She was looking straight at us.

"Are you talking to us?" I asked just to be sure the rules hadn't changed and she could see Lou and me.

No reply.

She couldn't see us.

"Miss," the woman said. "Can I help you?"

Lou looked bewildered. "I thought they couldn't see us."

I was about to say something when the woman spoke first.

"Pardon me?"

Grace, hidden behind Lou, poked her head out.

"Hello, dear one," the woman said waving at Grace. "She's a cutie, isn't she?"

Lou still didn't respond to the woman.

"Are you two lost? Why are you dressed so oddly?"

"She can see you, Lou." And I knew why. She really was a Never-was.

"How?"

"Miss?"

"No time to figure that out," I said. "You better say something to her or she's going to have you kicked out."

"What do I say?"

The woman looked around. "Are you talking to me?"

"Me?" Lou asked. "No... yes..."

"Are your parents guests at the house, miss?"

"My parents?"

"Lou," I said. "Get it together."

"Easy for you to say," she mumbled.

"Tell her..." I said, trying to think of a lie to get her out of this situation. I remembered the papers from the closet. "Tell her that Mr. Bashir sent you."

"Mr. Bashir sent me," Lou said.

The woman considered this new piece of information and then nodded. "He's sent you for lunch, hasn't he?"

"Ahhh..." was all Lou could manage to say.

"The grown-ups and their fancy inedible meals. I don't blame you. We've got the good stuff down here. Ham, cheese, macaroni, bread, and jam. You're welcome to join us in the staff dining room."

Lou looked at me for guidance.

"I suppose we should go," I said.

"Thank you," Lou said. "We'd like that."

The woman guided us through the hall, past what looked like a walk-in freezer and then through the kitchen. I entered the dining room ahead of the others. Four male staff members sat at the table enjoying sandwiches and milk. Their hands were speckled with dry white paint. A fifth person stood at the back of the room with his back to us. He was slumped over, picking through a pile of apples in a large bowl. I didn't need him to turnaround to know it was him. I could tell by the way he moved.

"I'm back," I said knowing that the other staff members couldn't hear me.

He half turned with a creepy smile on his face. "So you are," he said.

The other painters looked at each other, but quickly got back to their food. Clearly they were used to Fish's weird behavior. Seeing him talk to thin air was nothing new to them.

"I brought friends," I said.

He craned his neck a little more and saw Lou in the doorway. His smile grew a little bit bigger and then Throwaway Grace stepped past Lou. His smile faded quickly. "What..."

As if Grace knew the old man was tortured by her presence, she approached the old man and said, "Hello, Mr. Howard."

A painter at the table looked up from his meal and said, "Howard? Thought your name was Fish?"

Fish looked at the man with pure terror in his eyes. "You heard her?"

The painter flashed a half-toothed grin. "You're a nutty one, Fish. Bashir must have been half in the bag when he hired you."

"Bashir is as stupid as that mongoloid kid of his," the youngest of the painters said with a mouth full of ham sandwich.

"Here now," the woman who had shown us the way to the dining room said, "None of that talk. Mr. Bashir hears you talking like that he'll run you off the property with a pistol."

Fish had not taken his eyes off Grace.

I laughed. "This is where we make you pay."

"I've done nothing wrong!" Fish yelled.

The other painters looked startled by the obvious panic in his voice. One of them even went for the carving knife sticking out of the ham.

"Paint fumes have gotten to you, old man," the young painter said.

I chuckled. "This is just the beginning. The others are coming."

"No!" The old man grabbed the bowl of apples and flung it at me. It passed through me and struck the wall. Apples flew everywhere. He bolted out the back entrance to the dining room. I followed close behind. I heard the woman pleading with Lou and Grace to steer clear of Fish, but they emerged from the dining room shortly after.

Fish crashed through another door, and I could see the light from outdoors pour in. I let Lou and Grace catch up and we all exited the same door.

"What do we do?" Lou asked.

"He doesn't have the package with him," I said. "We've got to hope he leads us to it."

"What then? He's not just going to hand it to us."

"I'll distract him while and you and Grace grab it and take off."

"We can't separate," she said.

"We have to," I said. "Make your way back to the pool."

We followed Fish to a small row of stables. A half dozen horses wandered around a fenced-in area not far off. He walked as quickly as he could to a ladder leaned up against the side of one of the stables. A small wall of paint cans stood to the right of the ladder. He made his way around the cans and bent down out of sight. When he reappeared, he had the package in his hand.

"Hey," I barked. "It's over, Fish. Grace is just the first one. The others are coming."

"Shut up!" He backed away. "I sent them to heaven. They

couldn't have gone without me."

Throwaway Grace approached him without prompting from Lou or me.

"What is she doing?" Lou whispered.

"I don't know, but it's freaking the old man out, so I say we let her go with it."

"We appreciate everything you've done for us, Mr. Howard."

Fish's entire body was shaking. "I loved you all," he said.

"We know." Grace smiled. "That's why we're throwing you a party."

His expression changed from panic to relief in an instant. "A party?"

"Yes, sir," Grace said. "There's cake and punch." Approaching him, she reached out and took his free hand. "And plenty of sweet, sweet meat."

"A party for me? You're all such wonderful children."

"We've new tools for you," she said covering her mouth. "Oh, I've ruined the surprise. Now you know what your present is."

Fish laughed a sick and hardy laugh. "I won't tell."

"Thank you, Mr. Howard." She looked at us and smiled. "I promised everyone that you wouldn't bring your old tools with you."

The panic started to creep back into his face. "I can't leave my tools."

"But we've gotten you new ones. It will ruin everyone's fun if you bring the old tools. You don't want to ruin everyone's fun, do you, Mr. Howard?"

He thought it over. His eyes darted back and forth from the package of tools to Grace's face. "I wouldn't want to do that."

Grace squeezed his hand. "You can leave the package here. You won't need it anymore."

The old man hesitated, bent down, and carefully laid the

package on the grass.

"Everyone will be so pleased. Remember, you have to be surprised when you open your present," Grace said, leading the old man toward the woods that surrounded the stables.

"I will."

Lou started for them, but I grabbed her arm. "Don't move until they're out of sight."

"We can't let her just go off with him," she said.

"Just hold on," I said.

"But..."

I squeezed her arm. "This is the way it has to be."

She stopped resisting me and we both watched as Grace and the old man vanished into the woods. Once there were no signs of them, we ran to the package.

"That was insanely brilliant," I said. "I can't believe she did that. Did you talk to her?"

"No," Lou said. "I certainly wouldn't have told her to go off into the woods with the sadistic cannibal."

"Well, it worked."

"Just one thing," Lou said.

"What?"

"How do we get it back to our world without Grace? We need a Throwaway to bring it back."

Or a Never-was, I said to myself. "I may have been wrong about that," I said. "I think I'm the only one who can't be seen or interact with this world."

"That doesn't make sense," Lou said.

"Look where we are," I said. "Does any of this make sense? The staff in the mansion saw you but not me."

"Yeah, but that doesn't mean..." she bent down and reached for the package. Part of me wanted her hand to pass right through it. She was real. She had to be. Just as I convinced myself that she wasn't a Never-was, I saw her hand land gently, but solidly, on top of the canvas wrapped package. She screeched. "You were right. It must just be you."

I nodded. "Must be."

She picked up the package, and we heard a scream from the woods. "C'mon," she said running for the trees.

"No!"

"What?" she asked.

"We can't," I said.

"But that was Grace."

"Maybe," I said.

"That was Grace," she repeated in a tone that suggested that she could not be talked out of believing it.

"Listen," I said. "We have to get that package back to our world. That's the only thing that matters. If we leave the Land of the Dead without it, it's over."

"But..."

"Nothing else matters."

She looked at me with fire in her eyes. "I'm not leaving her."

I groaned. I was mad, but not at her. I was mad at me for being so willing to leave Grace behind. "I'll go after her. You get back to the pool."

She thought about arguing, but she knew deep down that I was right. The package mattered more than Grace. She kissed me on the cheek and said, "You better make it back."

I nodded and sent her on her way.

Entering the woods, it was easy to spot Fish and Grace's path. They had stomped their way through some pretty thick bush, breaking off limbs and leaving footprints along the way.

I reached a clearing and spotted something lying in the tall thick grass. The closer I go to it the more I realized that it wasn't just something. It was Grace. I picked up my pace and scanned the area for the old man as I ran. He was nowhere to be seen.

Kneeling down beside Grace, I saw her eyes flutter. She was alive, alive as a Throwaway could be. "Grace, are you okay?"

She didn't answer. She just smiled.

"Did he hurt you?"

She nodded.

"Where did he go?"

"He's gone to get his tools."

Her eyes started to close. "I'm taking you back."

She pushed herself away from me. "You have to find Lou before he does."

"I can't just leave you."

"I'll be okay." Her smile got bigger.

"Why are you smiling?"

"I got to be part of the story." With that, her eyes closed and her smile continued to grow.

I stood. "I'll come back," I said knowing in my gut that I wouldn't be able to return for her. "You were always part of the story. All of you." With that, I ran towards the mansion.

***

I stood on the edge of the pool looking for Lou. There was no sign of her. I was breathing heavily with my hands on my knees. My head felt like a lead weight. Every cell in my body ached from the sprint I had just completed. How could she not be here?

I glanced at the water and saw a dark object... no, two dark objects. It was Lou and the old man. He had her by the throat. Without a thought to my state of exhaustion, I dove into the pool, never taking into consideration that I was totally helpless in this world.

I swam at the old man and passed right through him. I turned and headed for him again. Lou kicked her way loose and swam for the surface. The old man did his best to go after her, but a current had hold of him and started to pull him back. I got caught in it, too. I even started to see Lou struggle against it.

Suddenly, the pool became pitch black, and I hit the ground with a crunching pop. I heard Lou moan in agony. We had made it out of the Land of the Dead.

I coughed and worked hard to breathe normally. "Lou, you okay?"

"Been better," she said.

The room, still dark, got bright enough for me to see her sitting up. "The package?"

She looked at me. "I don't have it."

DAY 9

TWENTY

"What do you mean you don't have it?" I said lying back down and covering my face with my hands. We were done without that package. We had one more day to make it back to the Land of the Dead and get the package to Detective King. That was the plan. Now we had nothing to deliver to the detective.

"I mean I don't have it," she said. I could hear her getting to her feet. "But that doesn't mean it's not here."

I sat up. "What?"

"I knew the old man was after me, so I hid it," she said.

I got to my feet. "You hid it?"

"I figured we didn't have to actually bring it back with us. If I hid it somewhere in the mansion, it would be waiting for us when we got back."

"You figured?" I asked sounding more than a little skeptical.

"It makes sense, right?"

"Where did you hide it?"

She headed for the shallow area of the pool, and I followed her hoping against hope that she figured right. She reached behind the ladder and popped out a screen to a filtering system. Her hand disappeared into the rectangular hole, and it seemed like an eternity passed before she pulled it out holding the package.

"Told you," she said.

"That was your hiding place?" I said in disbelief.

"It's not like I had a lot of time. I was lucky I found this spot."

We both climbed the ladder.

"Where's Ajax?" Lou asked as she stood waiting for me at the top of the ladder.

"Something's wrong," I said. "He wouldn't leave without a reason."

Lou took off running before I suggested we go looking for him. She headed directly for the bowling alley. Ariabod was gone, too. Gordy was propped up against the wall mumbling to himself. I kept my distance while Lou questioned him. I was so far away I couldn't make out what they were saying. I could tell that Gordy was on his last legs. He had lost a lot of blood, and he'd had nothing to eat or drink in days. He was sick. I could smell it.

Lou said one word that told me everything I needed to know about what was going on.

"Délons."

I could feel the blood rush through my veins. As soon as the word left her mouth, I could tell that they had been here. I could still feel their thoughts lingering in the air. I was still tuned into their collective.

"Ajax and Ariabod took on six of them in the basement."

"And?"

"And what?"

"Where are the dead Délons?" I asked.

"There aren't any. They fought for a while and then as suddenly as they arrived they retreated."

"That's not very Délon-like," I said.

"Maybe they're still here. Upstairs."

"No, they're gone. I'd know it if they were still here... Upstairs?" It came out like a question to her, but it wasn't. I was basically asking myself how I could be so stupid. "C'mon," I said, and we raced through the Halloween Room and headed for the stairs.

***

I couldn't bring myself to look at his face. Archie lay on a wooden table, still alive, but most likely wishing he was dead. The shunter attached to his face was sucking out his humanity.

Ajax and Lou signed to each other, while Kimball and Ariabod waited at the entrance to the fourth floor observatory.

Lou finished her conversation with Ajax and joined me by Archie's side.

"The six Délons in the basement were a decoy. They were sent down to keep Ajax and Ariabod busy while General Roy and his men came up here and took Bobby."

"What about Wes, Tyrone, and April?"

"They're alive. The Délons had no interest in them."

"They came for the Storyteller."

She nodded. "There's something else."

She handed me a note. "They left this note on Archie's body."

I took it from her and read it to myself. "Fulfill his destiny."

"What does it mean?" Lou asked.

I looked at the translucent jellyfish-like mass on Archie's face. I could see the unbearable pain leaking from his eyes. I thought back to the facility where I knew Archie as Scoop-face. His eyes and nose were missing. I did it to him. That's what he had said.

"I don't know what it means," I answered.

"We can't leave him like this," she said.

She was right, and I almost hated her for it. I wanted her to tell me that he wasn't our responsibility. That we should just leave him, but that's not why Lou was here. She was here to make sure I did the right thing no matter how wrong it felt.

"Take the gorillas and Kimball and check on the others. Let them know that this will all be over soon. They just have to hold out for one more day."

"What are you going to do?" She asked.

"Fulfill his destiny," I said.

She hesitated. When she said we couldn't leave him like this, she meant she wanted me to find a way to save him, but I knew that wasn't possible. I can't explain how, but I had been here before, hundreds of times maybe, and I had tried every way possible to save Archie, including ripping his face off and turning him into Scoop-face. I never succeeded, and Archie ended up paying dearly for my failed efforts. I wouldn't make him pay this time.

Lou left the observatory with the animals and I fought to keep from passing out. I didn't relish the thought of killing a man, especially a man who had helped me escape the facility and one I considered a friend. I pulled my hunting knife from my sheath and gripped it with a shaky hand.

"I wish there was another way, Archie." My voice cracked and changed pitch as I held back tears. "I don't want to do this."

I saw his eyes fixate on me.

"You are Creyshaw," I said gripping the knife with both hands and raising it above my head. I counted to three, took a deep breath, and fell to my knees in a blubbering mess. I couldn't do it. I couldn't kill him.

I felt a gentle tapping on my head. Startled at first, I backed away and then realized it was Archie patting me on the head. He motioned me to come closer. I did as asked, and he grabbed my hand holding the knife and guided it to his chest. I looked in his eyes and knew what he was telling me. I nodded, raised the knife over my head, and reminded myself out loud, "I am Creyshaw."

***

I threw-up three times after fulfilling Archie's destiny, which meant my stomach had less than nothing in it to keep me from starving to death. I was discovering that hunger is not only painful, but it's exhausting as well. I was so tired I barely had strength enough to descend the stairs. I stopped every ten steps or so and sat down to catch my breath.

I sat on the bottom step on the first floor and hung my head. I was so tired I had forgotten what was left for me to do. I knew I had one last trip to the Land of the Dead, but I couldn't remember why. It wasn't until I saw Lou approach with the package underneath her arm that I remembered.

"Detective King," I meant to say in full voice, but I wasn't capable of it. The words barely escaped my lips.

"We can't wait," Lou said. "Wes and Tyrone look worse than you. I couldn't even wake April up, and you saw Gordy. He's on death's door."

"Listen," I said, "if this doesn't work, you have to make sure that we don't get out of here."

"This will work."

"We don't know that. We don't even know if our next trip to the Land of the Dead will take us to King. This is the ninth day. If one of us gets out of here, we will infect the rest of what's left of this stupid world."

"What am I supposed to do, kill all of you?"

I didn't answer because she knew that was exactly what she was supposed to do.

"You can't ask me to do that," she said as the tears began to fall.

"I'm not asking you," I said. "I'm telling you. We're all weak from hunger. It wasn't supposed to happen this way. The Flish was expecting one of us to give in to temptation and take the others out. Eating them one by one. That would leave one infected individual strong enough to leave this mansion and spread his sickness across the globe. Instead he's got five strong-willed people barely able to stand. None of us will be able to put up a fight. Chain us up, and burn this place down with us inside."

"I'll be alone," she said sitting beside me. I could feel her trembling.

"No, you won't. You'll have Ajax, Ariabod, and Kimball. And you'll have a mission."

"What?" she asked wiping the corners of her eyes.

"Get that Délon picture to Tarek. He'll know what to do with it." With that, I leaned back and lay down on the steps. "I'm so tired."

I felt her shake me. "Don't go to sleep."

I turned to her, smiled, and closed my eyes.

***

I awoke to the sound of a horn honking. I opened my eyes and groaned as the glare from the sunlight seemed to zap my brain. After a while, I found the strength to sit up and examine my surroundings. The old-timey cars puttered up and down the busy street.

My hand shielding my eyes, I turned to the right and saw the dead boy crouched over me. I propped myself up on my elbows.

"I hope this is the right place," I said.

"It is," I heard Lou say excitedly. She was at the corner of the street. The people of the Land of the Dead were giving her strange looks for her choice of clothing. This time period didn't look too kindly on girls in pants, especially girls in jeans.

I stood up. "How do you know?"

"Because I heard that woman call that man Mr. King," she pointed to a man and woman down the street.

I approached and looked in the direction she was pointing. "That's him." I looked up at the street sign: East 52nd Street. As I panned down from the sign, I caught a glimpse of an elderly man approaching from two blocks away. Fish.

"We have to hurry," I said.

"Why?" She turned and answered her own question. "Crap."

A portly woman dressed in a fine blue dress gasped. "Such language."

Lou and I made a beeline for the detective.

"What do I say to him?" she asked. "He's going to think I'm nuts."

"Probably, but you just have to make him understand."

We reached the Detective and Lou was so nervous that she was out of breath. "Detective King."

The stout middle-aged man turned and looked at her with puffy blood-shot eyes. He looked as though he had not slept in years. He stared at Lou with a peculiar glare. "What is wrong with you, young lady, and how do you know my name?"

"Albert Fish," was all she said to make his eyes brighten.

"What about him? Do you know where he is?"

"Yes, sir. He's coming. We don't have much time."

"He's coming?"

"Listen to me," Lou barked. She was in a full-blown panic. She held out the canvas wrapped package. "This is his. It belongs to him."

The detective took the package from Lou. "What is it?"

"His tools."

"Tools?"

"I don't have time to explain. You can't let him have them. He gets his powers from his tools."

"Powers?" The detective laughed.

"He doesn't get it," Lou said to me.

"Who doesn't get what?" The detective asked.

"You're doing fine," I said.

She sighed. "These are your tools now, Detective King. You

can't let Fish get to them. Do you understand? If he gets his hands on this package, more kids will go missing. More kids will die. Do you understand?"

I saw something in his eyes change. If I was right, a little flash of light went off in his brain. He got it. He recognized that he would never understand completely why, but that package was his to watch over and protect. For a brief second, he seemed overwhelmed by the idea, but just as quickly something changed in him and he accepted it. That's when I knew for sure that he was the Keeper.

"I get it, kid. I'll never let it out of my sight."

Lou smiled. "You have no idea how important this is."

He smiled back. "I think I do."

TWENTY-ONE

We were all gathered around the table in the banquet room, Lou, Ajax, Ariabod, Wes, Tyrone, April, and Gordy. Kimball was lying down by my feet. Everyone except for Lou looked like death warmed over. She passed out the power bars and made sure we didn't devour them too quickly. She did the same with the water. We were all famished, but we were so weak we were having a hard time eating.

"It's over?" Wes asked.

"Must be," April said. "I don't want to eat any of you."

"Wish you felt that way a couple of days ago," Gordy said. He was the weakest of us all.

April put her hand over her mouth as if she just remembered what she had done. "Oh, God... I can't believe..."

Gordy snorted. "Relax. I don't blame you. I always knew you thought I was tasty."

April managed a smile.

"So what now?" Tyrone said.

"Tullahoma," Wes answered. "To look for more comic books."

I didn't say anything. I let them eat. As we gained our strength, we managed to actually enjoy each other's company. It was nice. It was needed. At one point, I saw Wes grab Lou's hand and gently squeeze it. His eyes were full of tears. She put her arm around his shoulder and kissed him on the cheek. I knew then that as much as I wanted to go home, I couldn't, not if it meant losing Lou.

I would rather spend my life surviving the end of the world with her then go back to living in normal times without her. Real or not, she was my one true love.

The End
of
Book Four

www.ingramcontent.com/pod-product-compliance
Lightning Source LLC
LaVergne TN
LVHW091043080826
845145LV00002B/602

* 9 7 8 0 9 7 9 2 0 6 7 3 3 *